WHERE LOVE LIVES: The Inheritance

Wyoming Wildflowers series

Book 6

Patricia McLinn

For news about upcoming books,
subscribe to Patricia McLinn's free newsletter.
www.PatriciaMclinn.com/newsletter

Wyoming Wildflowers series
Wyoming Wildflowers: The Beginning – Prequel (Snowberry)
Almost a Bride (Indian Paintbrush)
Match Made in Wyoming (Fireweed)
My Heart Remembers (Bur Marigold)
A New World (Prequel to Jack's Heart)
Jack's Heart (Yellow Monkeyflower)
Rodeo Nights (Prequel to Where Love Lives)
Where Love Lives (Threadleaf phacelia)

Dear Readers: If you encounter typos or errors in this book, please send them to me at Patricia@patriciamclinn.com. Even with many layers of editing, mistakes can slip through, alas. But, together, we can eradicate the nasty nuisances. Thank you! – Patricia McLinn

Layton, Felder, Bach & Moore
Attorneys-at-Law
58 East 42nd Street, Suite 1800
New York, New York 10016

Matt Halderman
683 Sage Ave.
Park, Wyoming, 82822

Dear Mr. Halderman,

I am acting as the executor of the estate of Mr. Harold
Hopewell, whose Last Will and Testament was entered
into probate in the Surrogate's Court, New York County,
State of New York. I write to inform you of certain
assets bequeathed to you pursuant to Mr. Hopewell's
Last Will and Testament, to wit:

A sum of money to execute the goal you discussed at
your first meeting and which he urged you to pursue.

I have enclosed a check for the full amount as well as
an envelope Mr. Harold Hopewell instructed should be
conveyed to you.

Please do not hesitate to contact me with any
questions.

Regards,
Frederick Bach, Esquire

CHAPTER ONE

"Did ya hear who's in town, Doc?"

Sometimes it took Zoe Parisi half a beat to realize "Doc" meant her.

She hadn't had that issue until she'd returned to Knighton, Wyoming, where "Doc" had meant Doc Johnson for as long as she could remember.

"No. Who?" she asked Earl Krenetz. What she really wanted to ask was how he'd heard anything about anybody, since this was his first trip to town in weeks.

He'd refused hospitalization for pneumonia, so until today she'd regularly trekked to his cabin, which clung to its mountain like one of those improbable trees springing from a rock crevice. She wouldn't miss that trip. From the clouds wrapping around the mountains it was snowing up there today, though it had only sleeted earlier today in Knighton.

Ah, Wyoming in April.

"Course, back in town's a figure of speech. Not in town at all." He laughed. Moving quickly, she caught another listen through the stethoscope, but then he picked up talking. "Getting things squared away on the place. Fencing first, which shows sense. Barn'll need a good bit of work. House, maybe."

Zoe wasn't surprised by Earl's priorities. A devotee of HGTV he was not.

"Used to come through now and then. But that ended a good while back and it hasn't been since … well, I don't know. Not precise. Hmmm, wonder when…"

If Earl fell into trying to figure "when," this conversation might never end.

Because "when" might hinge on its relationship to the year there'd been only two cuttings of hay, both bad, or the year after a dozen head died for no reason anyone ever did find, despite numerous efforts (each recounted in detail.) Or was it the year before? Could've been, but for sure it was after Gladys had twin calves, which ended up first and second at the county fair, though was it one or two years after?

"Who's in town?" she asked in a valiant effort to turn Earl's attention from "when."

No such luck.

"Long before the big change. Up and down for that family, that's for sure. Let's see … their people came into the county about 1890," he said as if he'd been here to see it.

Zoe got comfortable on the rollable stool. There would be no hurrying this. Her mind wandered to her schedule for the rest of the day as Earl recounted the end of the Nineteenth Century and the entirety of the Twentieth. He'd finally reached this century when she tuned back in.

"Couldn't have been easy seeing the family place after. That might be why he stopped coming back. Course that was after his mama married that Cartwright fella from Colorado."

A voice—*his* voice—came into her head.

She married this ass named Cartwright from Denver. Did she really remember that? No. Had to be her imagination, not her memory. No reason that would stick with her for years. Not when she hadn't let the rest of it stick with her.

That night…

That one night…

"And then he hit it big." Earl chuckled. "Not the way he'd hoped as a young'un, of course, but with a whole lot fewer broken bones I'd wager."

Zoe shifted from a tickle at the back of her neck. It wasn't the kind of tickle that made her want to laugh.

There was no reason on earth he'd be in Knighton. She'd made absolutely sure before she'd—

"Who?"

Earl blinked at her no-fooling around demand. "Matt Halderman. Who else would I be talkin' about? Grew up on the H Bar H Ranch up the highway like I'm telling you. Not far from the spread Taylor and Cal Ruskoff have. Malloys have the H Bar H now, but it was the Haldermans' for generations. Young Matt started rodeoing as a boy here. Though it wasn't his ridin' that's made him rich. Story I heard is—"

But Zoe didn't want to hear this story or any story concerning Matt Halderman. She wanted the answer to one question: "Why? Why is he here?"

No, make that two questions, but she wasn't going to ask Earl how soon before Matt Halderman left.

"What do you mean, why, Doc? He's come home is why."

Doc Johnson looked up as Zoe entered the clinic's sole office.

He came in part-time now, but she'd insisted he keep the big old desk he loved. She had a smaller one in a corner.

"We lost that physician's assistant recruit to Denver," he announced immediately.

They'd been trying to hire a physician's assistant or a nurse practitioner or both for the clinic with no success.

"The money or the isolation?"

"Both. How's Earl?" he asked.

"Better. Good progress. You should be able to pull up his chart."

Doc used one finger to type in the name. He wasn't speedy, but he was sure. "No matter how he is, you're not taking any more trips up that mountain of his, you understand?"

"With the telemedicine program, I wouldn't have to."

"*Hah.* You don't have to win me over to that program, but don't try to fool me. You'd still be going up. When your grandmother told me what you'd been doing, taking him groceries and… Uh-huh. Uh-huh. Yup." The chart had distracted him from that well-worn discussion. "Looks like he's over that pneumonia for sure. I figured that when I heard him in the waiting room talking nineteen to a dozen about Matt Halderman being in town."

"Just passing through?" She tried to keep hope out of her voice.

"Not from what I hear. Bought a piece of the H Bar H. I'd imagine he wanted the whole thing.

He had.

She didn't say that aloud, giving only a noncommittal *hmm*.

"Malloys must be settled in good there because he sure could pay top dollar nowadays. Hometown boy makes good. You know the story, don't you?" Like Earl, Doc needed no encouragement. "He was still on the rodeo circuit, then one night he starts talking to this fella in a truck stop. Turns out the guy's a billionaire. Can you imagine that? By lunch the billionaire plunked down the money right then and there to bring out this travel app Matt created. Guess it was all that traveling from rodeo to rodeo that gave him the idea. Been doing real well from everything you hear."

Zoe had done her best *not* to hear. Not everything, not *anything* when it came to Matt Halderman. She'd made it a practice, like brushing her teeth or washing her hands. It had served her well for years.

Until now, perhaps.

"Few years go by, with Matt building that company of his and then the billionaire dies," Doc Johnson said. "He left Matt money in his will."

Why couldn't this unknown billionaire have left the money to her? Or to Doc? Or to any of another half dozen people in Knighton who'd immediately fund their participation in the telemedicine program. Not only would it benefit so many people in Lewis and Clark counties, but if the billionaire had left the money to them, he wouldn't have left it to Matt Halderman and he wouldn't have come back to Knighton. Talk about a win-win.

"Nobody says how much," Doc went on, unaware of her dark thoughts about the ways of billionaires, "but it must have been a good amount, because Matt turns around and buys up that land like I told you. Taylor's been acting for him. Dave for the Malloys."

Taylor Anne Larsen Ruskoff was one of Knighton's two lawyers.

Zoe's grandmother commanded the office of the other lawyer in town—Dave Currick.

"Remember Matt as a boy, always pushing the limits—had him here regular with injuries," Doc Johnson said.

Growing up, Zoe had spent summers and holidays with her grandparents in Knighton. She had often been an anonymous face in the awed audience of kids for those limit-pushing episodes. Some successful, some not.

"But not crazy foolish. Never that kind of wild. Not until his dad died. Then… Especially when his mother and that second husband of hers took him off to Montana." Doc shook his head. "All kinds of trouble he got into."

Phil Halderman had died when Zoe wasn't in Knighton. By her next visit, Matt, his mother, and her new husband were gone.

She hadn't seen Matt for years.

Until that night…

Doc Johnson chuckled. "Took rodeo to calm him down. Why, I remember one time…"

CHAPTER TWO

Matt sat in the lawyer's office, listening to a rundown on work completed on the property he'd named Pegasus Ranch.

"The men you hired did a good job on the fences," Taylor Anne Larsen said.

He'd put out a call for hard-working rodeo cowboys needing to earn a stake to get back on the circuit. They were highly motivated.

"They spoke highly of both of you, too." He looked at Taylor, the lawyer who'd handled arrangements. Then to her husband, Cal Ruskoff, who'd overseen the work. "Appreciate all you did. What you both did."

"Fences are good and solid now," Cal said. "Wouldn't say the same for the barn."

"That'll come. I also appreciate your coming to town today so this could all be done at once, Cal. Less time I spend in town, less talk there will be."

"You *have* been away from Knighton for a long time," Taylor said with a small smile as she put another paper in front of him to sign.

"Oh, I remember well enough to guess eighty percent of the town knew my business before I'd brought my truck to a full stop outside your office."

At least some of his business. Not even his lawyer knew the plan for the next phase. He'd kept that close to the vest. He'd learned that from the best in rodeo, Walker Riley. "Poker and life, only show your cards to folks you're sure are on your side and going to stay there."

Taylor swapped out the signed paper for another form. Then another and another.

He'd gone through these beforehand, working out details back and forth through calls, emails, texts, and such. Communications at the ranch would be rudimentary for a while, so better to do the signing in person.

He checked the time. They'd be pulling in soon.

"What's that you're humming?" Taylor asked.

His signing hand paused. "Old song called 'Where Love Lives.' Friend of mine arranged so it played a lot while I was driving here." By making an entire playlist that one song. Over and over it played. Kalli Evans Riley had a way of making her point even when she wasn't standing in front of him.

"I thought I recognized it. That's a great song. The house has been cleaned and basics moved in as you requested." Taylor looked up at him from the stack of signed papers she was compiling. "*Very* basic."

"Basic's fine. Thank you, Taylor."

"Maybe for a while, but really, Matt…"

"Barn's next," he said firmly.

"Speaking of which, here's the itemized estimate for supplies for what I'm thinking you'll need to fix the barn." Cal handed him multiple pages. That couldn't be good.

It wasn't. The list of needed material starkly told the extent of deterioration. And these dollar amounts didn't even touch on labor costs.

A tap sounded on the slightly ajar office door. It started to open wider. A woman's voice came. "Taylor, that new assistant you hired isn't out front. Do you have a—"

The door swung wide enough for him to see the new arrival.

He couldn't put it together for a second.

In his memories, she wasn't wearing a jacket over pressed jeans and boots.

In his memories, she wasn't wearing anything.

And she wasn't unexpectedly standing in the doorway of his lawyer's office.

She was in his bed.

Sleeping, as he took one last look before he closed the door behind him.

And now here she was. He'd thought maybe someday—But it was too soon. He wasn't ready.

She took a second step in then stopped dead, spotting him.

He spoke first.

"*You.* What are you doing here?"

His words weren't much. His tone was.

Plenty enough to make Cal half rise from his chair, perhaps with the intention of stepping between him and Zoe.

Matt could have assured the other man he was no threat to Zoe Parisi … if he could have gotten another word out.

Taylor stretched her hand toward her husband. He sank back to the chair, but didn't settle.

"I didn't know you knew Zoe, Matt," she said calmly. "But now that you'll be living here, of course you'll cross paths a lot. She's the best thing to happen to this area in ages. Oh, what was I thinking? You probably knew each other as kids from when she'd visit Hugh and Ruth."

"Yes," Zoe said.

He said at the same time, "No."

"Uh-huh," Taylor said neutrally. "Well, as I said, you'll be crossing paths a lot, so let's make sure there's no confusion: Zoe Parisi, this is Matt Halderman, the newest landowner in Lewis County." She gestured to the signed papers on her desk. "Matt, this is Zoe Parisi, our new doctor."

"Doctor," he repeated.

She made it.

She'd been so determined and she'd done it. Over any and every obstacle that came her way. He felt an inexplicable swell of warmth inside his chest.

She lifted her head. "Yes."

The warmth flash-froze.

She wasn't just a doctor. She was the doctor *here.*

In Knighton.

"Temporary?" That came out half-choked. "Filling in for Doc Johnson or—"

"Oh, no," Taylor said. "Zoe's taking over from Doc Johnson. They've been working together for a while. He told me the other day that he could retire any time and rest comfortable with Zoe in charge."

"I'm staying." Zoe's "*I'm*" had a touch of emphasis to it.

He heard it. And answered it. "That so? Well, I am, too." He thunked his hand on the stack of papers. "It's official. Here to stay."

Her gaze went to the papers. She licked her lips as if they'd suddenly gone dry.

He wished she hadn't done that. He really wished she hadn't.

He remembered that mouth. That sweet, sweet mouth.

Heat abruptly and painfully attacked his flash-frozen insides.

"Sorry to have barged in when you're doing business, Taylor. I'll talk to you later. Cal." Zoe said nothing more to him. Didn't even look at him.

She turned and left, tugging the door closed as she went. But it didn't latch.

Before he knew he intended to, he'd stood.

"I, uh… Excuse me a minute." He went after her.

From the corner of his eye he saw Cal half rise and Taylor again make a gesture for him to stay.

Matt pulled the office door closed behind him. Zoe was across the outer office, nearly to the outside door.

"Zoe."

She paused.

"I didn't mean…"

She faced him. "Didn't mean what?"

"Didn't mean to catch you off guard like this." Judging from the flash in her eyes, his words hadn't quelled her irritation. More like stoked it. Well, hell, he'd been caught off guard, too. "Look, I had no idea you were in Knighton. I mean, I knew you'd thought about it from what you said that ni—From what you said. But I didn't know you were a real doctor, much less that you'd come back here to practice."

She straightened. "Never thought I could do it, huh? Well, I did."

"That isn't—" He combed his hair back with his fingers. "I know this is awkward, but it's not like we had a commitm…"

That was the wrong path to follow. He knew that. Doubted he'd get any points for not having finished the word.

But where the hell was a better path? Every direction showed gaping pitfalls.

"Don't worry, Matt," she said in a voice that would have worried him if it weren't already sending renewed ice through his veins. This shifting back and forth from freezing to heat was brutal. "There was no question of a commitment or any semblance of a claim on each other. And I have no interest in changing that."

She straightened, coming as tall as she could, though still not much more than to his shoulder. She was paler. In his memories, she'd been tanned from the summer outdoors. Was she not getting outside enough now? Not taking care—

"In fact, let me be very clear." Her voice was so cold he'd swear he heard ice tinkling in it. "I don't want anything from you now except your money."

CHAPTER THREE

He actually took half a step backward.

Good.

But he recovered fast. Too fast.

Then the flicker of a grin appeared. Smug. That's what that grin was. *Smug.* And thank heavens it was, because it dialed back his appeal several notches.

"Well," he said, "at least you're honest about being after money. What makes you think I'd give you any?"

"It's not a matter of giving me—"

"Oh, you think I owe you?" There was no doubting his tone. He made her sound like—something she wasn't.

As if she hadn't kicked herself sufficiently already for giving in to desire that one night, he'd just made her want to kick herself all over again.

Hold on a minute.

No, *not* kick herself. She wanted to kick *him.*

Somewhere that would hurt a lot for a long, long time. Her medical knowledge gave her several excellent options. Stopping to decide on one slowed her enough to let reason take hold.

With precise pronunciation, she said, "The money's not for me. It's for the people of Lewis and Clark counties."

"How's that?"

"For less money than you must have spent on that land, we can set up a program that would make telemedicine available here. Both for me to consult with folks who live way out, and for me and patients to connect with specialists. Right at our fingertips instead of sending people hundreds and hundreds of miles away, hoping you're sending them to the right specialist and—"

She broke off. She was going on too long.

"The community is raising money. The problem is we need it now—at least by the end of next month—to get signed up for the next twelve months. Otherwise we'll have to wait a full year and there are people who shouldn't have to wait. Who can't wait.

"That money would let us access real-time video consultations with some of the top experts in more specialties than you can imagine. Emergency medicine and patient monitoring. I'd be the hands, but they'd be the expertise and cutting edge knowledge and—"

"I get it." The grin she didn't like was back, now accompanied by a drawl. "You've got plans for my money. Well, I've got plans for it, too."

"*Your* money," she scoffed. "It fell in to your lap. Dropped from the sky. Like picking up a tossed lottery ticket then finding out it's a winner. That money wasn't part of your planning."

"It is now. And the trouble—from where you're standing—is I already spent it."

He'd snapped the first three words. Then he'd shifted to a tone so falsely sympathetic she was back to thinking of places to hurt him.

"On what? A vacation home? A ranch you'll jet into for a weekend now and then like those movie stars in Montana? Someplace to get away from it all and relax after your stressful life?"

Another grin. "Sort of like that. Not the movie stars jetting in for the weekend part, but that last part. Get away from it all and relax. That's it. Only it's not just for me." He cocked his head, listening, and she became aware of a rumble outside. "And if I'm not mistaken, here come our first residents."

He went past her, opening the outside door.

The sound of truck engines came louder. She caught a glimpse of a semi cab slowly approaching along Main Street. But her view of what it pulled was blocked by Matt's broad shoulders when he stopped just outside the door.

She tried to circle around him, but a far skinnier male form blocked that angle.

Deputy Sheriff Duane Jessup.

Great. Just great.

He hadn't spotted her. That was at least a temporary relief.

He frowned at the pickup truck with a two-horse trailer attached parked right in front of these offices. She should have noticed that on her way in, but she'd been so focused on getting information from Taylor that would prepare her for seeing Matt…

Yeah, that went well.

"This your truck?" Jessup demanded of Matt.

"Yes, it is."

"What do you think you're doing?"

Matt didn't look at Jessup. "I'm watching those trucks coming in to town."

"Parking here, I mean. You can't be pulling head first into a spot like this with a horse trailer on the back."

"Don't worry, I can back out fine with that small trailer." He started down the wood steps to street level.

"That's not—Zoe. Hi."

She was aware of Matt stopping on the steps and turning back toward them.

Since Jessup had spotted her, there was no benefit to staying in the doorway. She started along the sidewalk, intending to keep going.

Jessup stepped in front of her.

"Deputy?"

Matt returned up the steps. The deputy didn't seem to notice.

Jessup said, "You look real pretty today, Zoe."

The man's arm came up as if to touch her hair. She stepped back.

Matt wrapped a hand around her wrist and tugged her toward him. "You want to see these new arrivals, so c'mon, Zoe."

Continuing the momentum of his move reversed their positions, which landed Jessup's stroke on Matt's upper arm.

"Watch it," Matt said, low.

He started her down the steps.

"I'm going to have to write you a ticket," Jessup proclaimed, trailing after.

"Do what you gotta do, Deputy."

"Don't make an issue of this," Zoe said under her breath. For her sake or his?

He looked down at her. "No issue. No problem." Then, louder, he called to the driver of the first of two trucks, each a semi cab hauling a giant horse trailer. "How'd it go, Lee?"

"Not bad. If you like hauling devils in horsehide. Fortunately, I do."

"You've got about another fifteen miles to go," Matt said. "Unless you want to stop to water them now?"

"Naw. They're good for that."

Matt gave them directions. "I'll be there right after you."

"I've given you a ticket," Jessup announced from behind them as the trucks began to roll forward again.

Abruptly aware Matt still held her arm, Zoe stepped away.

The deputy went on, "If you think you can ignore it because you're some big—"

"I won't ignore it."

Zoe jumped in. "Those trailers are enormous. How many horses are you bringing in?"

"This first run, fifteen total."

They were standing close enough and the trucks were going slow enough that they caught sight of several of the passengers.

"That's the sorriest bunch of horseflesh I've seen this side of the glue factory." Jessup clearly intended that to be insulting.

He must not have looked at the horses in the trailer behind Matt's pickup, because what Zoe had seen of them was impressive.

"That's the point," Matt said.

Jessup sneered. "You're going to slaughter old horses?"

Zoe sucked in a breath.

Matt's voice remained level and cool. "No. We're going to treat them right. Give them comfort and protection in their last years. Let them die as easy as they can."

"A *hospice?*" Zoe was surprised not only at what he was doing, but also that she had spoken. "You're running a *horse* hospice."

He turned to her, his brown eyes bright. "That's a good way of saying it. A horse hospice. I like that. We're going to try, anyway."

CHAPTER FOUR

Zoe had work to do. She did not have time for memories.

Not memories of how many ways this afternoon had gone wrong. From walking in on him in Taylor's office, to the shock on his face, to blurting out that she wanted his money.

Not memories of childhood summers when he'd seemed to glow with a special aura all his own.

Not memories of that night…

One night when their paths had crossed in a way that her starry eyes had seen as destiny.

Oh, yeah, she'd thought she'd been so grown up. She'd even thought she'd seen a reflection of herself as a desirable, alluring woman in his eyes.

Even though he didn't remember her.

Certainly not when he'd first opened the door of her room at that bed and breakfast on the other side of the state. She couldn't blame him for not knowing her then. All she'd worn were towels—one around her hair, the other covering from shoulder to knees—after a gloriously hot shower that had made up for two weeks' deprivation.

She almost hadn't recognized him, which she would never have expected. But disappointment, pain, exhaustion and something darker had shifted the planes of his face, making it less handsome, yet even more heart-clenching.

"What the hell are you doing in my room?" he'd demanded.

"I'm in *my* room," she'd shot back.

That's how it had started.

How it had ended was waking to find a four-word note: *Wish you the best.* Signed with the letter M.

She'd been a stupid kid.

Or a delusional idiot.

She preferred stupid kid. At least that sounded more hopeful, because it could mean that in the intervening years, as she'd earned her medical degree and learned a whole lot beyond medicine, she'd changed.

Delusional idiot sounded scarily permanent.

Lee and the others had not only unloaded the horses, but had helped Matt sort and settle them.

He fed Roo, his favorite roping horse, another apple slice before turning him into the pasture that would be his new home.

"That's it for now, buddy."

He'd seriously underestimated the need for apples. Apple juice, too.

Eventually he'd have to go to Jefferson for more supplies for man and beast. But that could wait a week, easy. Apples and apple juice couldn't.

Maybe the diner in Knighton could fix him up.

He called and in five minutes had a "sure, I remember you" from the waitress Rainie and a promise of what he needed by the day after tomorrow. That would work.

So he'd be going back into Knighton.

Where Zoe Parisi lived.

Wasn't that a kick in the… Well, take your pick of body parts.

He knew which one had reacted first to seeing her, but that wasn't a good one to go by. He'd finally learned that lesson with too many of the wrong kind of female.

How many times had Walker and Kalli Riley indicated he was roping in the wrong pen if he wanted a real relationship? Then again, few had a relationship like they did.

They'd like Zoe Parisi.

Now, where the hell had that thought come from? Like they'd ever meet her, considering her reaction to him today.

As for his reaction…

Someday, maybe, but… It was too soon. He wasn't ready.

He'd been caught by surprise was all. It wasn't like he'd pursued these goals for the sole purpose of impressing Zoe Parisi. No. He was doing what he needed to do for himself.

As for her…

I don't want anything from you now except your money.

Her scorn was not subtle. He kind of liked that. No need to guess what she was thinking. Or what she wanted.

She wasn't the first to want his money. Though it was novel that she wasn't after bangles—or, in one case, houses, international travel, and unlimited spending money.

It had also been novel that she'd broken off her words instead of trying to talk him into submission.

Wouldn't have mattered if she had tried to.

God knows he respected her pursuing her goals. But he had his own now, too. Harold Hopewell had referenced that in his handwritten note enclosed in the lawyer's letter. The note saying how Harold wanted him to use the inheritance.

He wasn't going to turn his back on that request. No way.

That's why he'd interrupted her.

It didn't matter how enthusiastic, how compelling, how persuasive she might be. She had her mission. He had his.

And the trouble—from where you're standing—is I already spent it.

At least the first part of it. To get things started. The rest was set aside for the next step.

He looked out across a landscape sounding the first, sweet, teasing notes of spring. And beyond, to where it swept up to a peaked horizon enclosing the only place on earth he wanted to be.

"Step one, Dad," he said aloud.

Roo pricked his ears at the low tone he clearly recognized.

Matt patted him. "No chute opening this time, buddy."

This time the fight wasn't in the arena. And it would be a while, possibly a long while, before he could say, "We did it, Dad."

… But she had.

Zoe Parisi had done exactly what she'd said she'd do that night.

That night…

"I'm going to be a country doctor."

No doubt, no wavering.

She'd just completed a two-week wilderness first aid training course. That was her break from school and working. Her vacation. Taking a course in the rough so she'd know how to help people.

"Why?" he'd asked.

"Because people need medical care. Especially people who aren't in cities or big towns. The lack of medical care for rural patients is at a crisis level. There have to be new ways of thinking. They desperately need doctors. More and more doctors go into specialties and fewer and fewer go to rural areas."

"And you're going to fix all that." He'd said it a little teasing, but not because he doubted her. Maybe he'd teased because he didn't doubt her.

"All of it, no." She'd said that with regret. "But I can fix one small part of it. I'm going to."

He'd kissed her then. Kissed her, then made love to her a second time.

And a third.

Now here she was. In Knighton. Dr. Parisi. Doing what she'd been so sure she needed to do. With a certainty that had made him look at himself in the mirror that night.

And had changed his life.

CHAPTER FIVE

"Oh, good, Matt, you came into town to help us with Beautify Knighton Day," Matty Brennan Currick said from beside Zoe.

Zoe's head jerked up and cracked against the bottom of the window box frame beneath the diner's front window.

"Ouch," Matty said sympathetically to her. They had the window box insert on the sidewalk in front of them to plant with flowers as their part to prepare Knighton's Main Street for summer. "That had to hurt."

"It's okay," she lied as she rubbed the spot on her head.

"Maybe you should have a doctor check it." Even without looking at Matt, she knew he was grinning as he said that.

"No need." She stood, pretending she wanted another marigold to add to the planter's mix. Standing didn't make her the same height as him but at least it left her at less of a deficit than sitting cross-legged on the sidewalk.

"Maybe not, but you're going to need a hair washer if you don't quit grinding in that dirt."

She jerked her hand away from her head. The gardening glove that covered that hand did look suspiciously cleaner than the other one. She brushed at her hair and flecks of dirt sprayed out.

"More over to this side." Matt brushed at her hair.

She stepped away from the touch. But that meant she could see him better. A faded blue plaid shirt that had to be creating an optical illusion of shoulders that broad, belt with a modest rodeo buckle, snug fitting jeans sliding along muscled legs, boots, and a straw cowboy hat.

She gestured to the last item. "Pushing the season, aren't you? It snowed in the mountains again yesterday."

"Power of positive thinking."

Matty, still sitting, looked up from her to Matt and back. She was older than them, but had grown up here, too, eventually marrying her childhood sweetheart Dave Currick. "So you two already know each other?"

"No," Zoe said.

"Yes," he said.

Matty's eyes lit up. "Oh, ho. Now that sounds interesting."

Their eyes met for an instant. Taylor had been too discreet to push for an explanation of their varying answers the other day in her office. No way would Matty let it go. To get past her curiosity they needed to cooperate.

"When I used to visit my grandparents here on vacations as a kid, I knew who Matt was from around town, but he was older. Part of the cool crowd."

"No, was I?"

She ignored his delighted question. "He and his friends never noticed any of the little kids trailing along after them for as long as they'd tolerate it. Eventually, they'd shoo the whole lot of us away."

"I don't know about that last part, but I must have noticed you or I wouldn't have said yes, that we knew each other before, would I?"

His eyes glittered with challenge and a hint of amusement at her predicament.

She certainly wasn't going to introduce their more recent history to explain their differing answers, so her best alternative was to accept his explanation in hopes of satisfying Matty.

Who, at the moment, was displaying great interest.

"How can I possibly know what you noticed? I can only go by your actions."

There, that dimmed the amusement in his eyes.

Good.

She dropped back to the sidewalk and jammed the marigold in to place.

"His actions show he's civic-minded by coming to join the effort to beautify Knighton for the summer. Assuming it ever gets here," Matty said. "Grab a trowel."

"Actually, I—"

"Oh, Matt, I was hoping I might see you today." It was Taylor. She paused for smiling hellos to the two women, then added, "How are things at Pegasus Ranch? Are you making out okay?"

"Just fine. Except I was running low on a couple things and Rainie kindly said she'd get them in for me today so I don't have to go to Jefferson."

"So *not* civic minded," Zoe said, half under her breath.

"But now that you're here, you can help out," Matty said to him.

Zoe often admired the older woman's persistence. Not at the moment, however.

Especially not when, after moment's pause, he said, "Sure. I can help for a while. What do you need?"

"You can put this liner back into the box—we're done, don't you think, Zoe? And take down the next one for us. And another bag of potting soil from the stack over by the drugstore. Taylor, you can—"

"Oh, no you don't, Matty. You're not shanghaiing me. I've finished my office and now I'm going down to the library to help Cal. I just stopped by to say hello and check in with Matt. I'll go with him as far as the potting soil, then I'm on my way."

He set the next window box liner down in front of them, and he and Taylor left. Zoe began planting this liner to match the first.

"Dave and I'll have to get over there to see Pegasus Ranch and welcome him properly," Matty said. "Have you been there?"

"No." She said it too shortly, but at least she didn't add the overtly defensive, *Why would I?* that almost followed.

Matty didn't seem to notice. "Must be strange for him, being back on his family's ranch, now that it's not his family's ranch."

She sold it. He was hardly in the ground and she just sold the ranch that had been in our family for generations.

Zoe heard his voice in her memory. The two of them sitting up in the big bed, his arm around her shoulders, his other hand clasped in both of hers. The dimness around them making all things possible.

Never asked me. Never considered how I'd feel about it. And when I told her, she laughed. That laugh everybody told her was so damned musical. Said she wanted a better life. Better.

She'd felt such sorrow for him then, listening to words taut with scars a dozen years old then. Now pushing two decades old. Did he feel the loss as strongly?

Matty was looking at her. What had Matty just said? Something that required a response… Oh, right. About it being weird for him having a piece of the H Bar H, but not the whole.

"I suppose. But it was his choice. He could have gone anywhere. Anywhere in the world." A little bitterness edged in that he hadn't gone anywhere else in the world. Zoe reined it in. "With that business he started being such a success and then a billionaire leaving him a pile of money, I mean."

She'd heard more about that in the days since Doc Johnson had given her the bare outline. A lot more.

His company was some huge success that had been written up in business and tech magazines. And then, on top of it, Harold Hopewell left him money. No one knew the amount, but everyone agreed it had to be plenty.

"Sure he could have gone anywhere. Shows his good sense that he came back home."

"Who came back home?" asked a new voice.

Zoe and Matty turned to see Val Trimarco standing behind them. Across the street, Jack Ralston was entering the drug store carrying her daughter, Addison Rose. That seemed fair since Val was carrying his baby in a discreet baby bump. A wedding was being planned to formalize what everyone could see—they were a family.

"Where's Jack going?" Matty asked.

"To get Addie chocolate ice cream." Val sighed, blending exasperation and fondness. "Not only did he give in before I could even say no, but *chocolate*. After she insisted on wearing her yellow top. I can't stand to watch. So who came home?"

"I expect that was me," answered a deep voice.

It shouldn't have been so familiar so fast. Wouldn't have been if Zoe hadn't heard it in her head so often these past years.

She turned to see Matt with three bags of soil balanced on one shoulder. He swung them down together, landing them with a thud on the sidewalk. He rubbed his hand on the side of his jeans and extended it to Val.

"Matt Halderman."

"Val Trimarco. This is only my second summer here but I don't remember seeing you before."

"It's a long story," he said. "I'd be happy to share it with you some evening."

Zoe kept her head down.

"Along with my guy, my daughter, and a slew of friends, I'd be delighted. Otherwise, no way, cowboy," Val said with good humor.

"Can't blame a guy for trying."

Zoe knew without looking that he was grinning that grin she'd first seen when he'd been a pre-teen showing off for all the kids.

"Val might not blame you for trying, but Jack will," Matty said with a chuckle. Jack Ralston was foreman for the combined operation of her family ranch and her husband's family ranch. "Besides, Val, there's something between Matt and Zoe. Matt grew up on the H Bar H. You know, on the way to Cal and Taylor's place. Matt, this is Val, who gave birth to her daughter in a blizzard here a few years back, then returned last summer and created the Jack you see today."

"No way. He did it himself. Maybe with some help from Addison Rose—that's my daughter," she told Matt. "But what's this about something between you and our Dr. Z?"

"Matty's imagination. There's nothing—" Zoe began.

"It all started in childhood," Matt said at the same time.

Matty stood. "I *knew* there was something between the two of you. And *not* from childhood. Chemistry."

Zoe was going to shoot the man.

The only thing that saved him now was the infectious giggle of a little girl.

Still seated, Zoe turned to see Addison Rose Trimarco—soon to be Addison Rose Trimarco-Ralston, and if there ever was a child to carry off that amount of name, this was the girl to do it—arriving in the arms of a smiling Jack Ralston.

Seeing him smile still took some getting used to. Val had done him a world of good. Along with Addie.

"This must be Val's daughter I've heard so much about." Matt sounded just a little uneasy. Good.

"*Our* daughter." There was no mistaking Jack's tone.

"Is okay, Jack." Addie patted a chocolate encrusted hand on his cheek. "He's new."

That eased any discomfort amid stifled chuckles.

Introductions were made all around by Matty and Val.

"Where's Dave?" Jack asked. "Thought he'd be helping you."

"Still working on his office. He tried to just dump plants still in their containers in a couple pots and Ruth found out. So he has to re-do everything. Least that's the rumor on the street." Matty's grin was evil. "Better yet, we worked out a deal that he'd look after the kids as long as he was working on his office."

"Down, Jack. Pease," Addie requested.

In a second, a curious face under a mass of dark curls was beside Zoe. "Whatchya doin'?"

"Planting flowers."

"Yellow monkeyflower?"

Matty, Val, and Jack chuckled. Zoe and Addie turned toward them. Along with amusement, Val and Jack were sharing a look that should persuade Matt or any man with a lick of sense that he had no chance on earth with Val Trimarco.

"What's so funny?" Zoe asked.

"Nothing." Possibly realizing she had not been at all convincing, Val quickly addressed her daughter. "Yellow monkeyflower needs more room to grow than they have in window boxes, Addie. That's a marigold, like Cousin El, Cahill, and Sam plant in the Inn's herb garden in Gloucester."

"Oh." The girl nodded wisely.

"Gloucester's where—" Val started.

"I can tell Dr. Zoe. I can tell," Addie announced. "El and Cahill and Sam are my family. I have *lots* of family. I have family here. I have family in Gloucester. That's in Massa*cheesits*. By the ocean."

Zoe bit the inside of her mouth to keep from laughing at the girl turning the state into a snack food. "That sounds lovely. What a lucky girl to have family in two places."

A new female voice arrived from behind where Zoe and Addie sat. "Jack, Val, so glad you're here. You're assigned down by—*Oh*."

That long, drawn out breath of appreciation informed Zoe that Joyce Aberdick, assistant manager of the bank, had just spotted Matt.

It was only partly about his looks. The other part was that Joyce loved to talk about people. Not maliciously, necessarily, but definitely to spread the word about other people's activities. Matt Halderman represented prime, fresh talking material.

Didn't hurt he was prime in other areas, too.

Matty made quick introductions.

Zoe occupied herself with showing Addie how she was planting the mix of flowers, making sure their roots had room and holding the plant upright while the girl patted soil in place around the stem. A little dried chocolate ice cream never hurt a plant.

"We better get going," Val said after a while. "We promised Cal we'd help at the library. Lots of planting to do there."

Turning to wave good-bye to Addie, Val, and Jack, Zoe saw Joyce step closer to Matt as she peppered him with questions. He backed up a step.

Zoe grinned to herself.

"Poor man," Matty murmured, looking in the same direction. "We'll have to rescue him."

Zoe was saved from saying "No way," when Rainie stepped out of the diner. The long-time waitress knew more than Joyce about the town's goings on and repeated little.

"Quit distracting the help, Joyce," Rainie ordered. "Matt, your things are by the back door. When you're ready, pull your truck around there."

"I can do that now—"

"Oh, no," Matty interrupted. "I need you to go get us more plants. At least three more flats. The same mix as here."

"I don't know one flower from another. I'd—"

"No problem. Zoe, you go with him," Matty ordered. "That way he can carry back two and you bring one flat and none will get squashed."

"I—"

"Go, go," Matty ordered. "And Joyce, you sit down here and take Zoe's place."

"I can't. I can't get dirty. I'm going into Jefferson after this."

Zoe jumped on that. "Have Joyce go with him for the flats and I'll stay here."

"I'm just organizing today, not planting," Joyce said.

"Everybody gets dirty on Beautify Day," Rainie snapped.

"I don't see you digging in the dirt," Joyce complained.

"That's because you weren't here before dawn to see me pulling out the old plants and washing these flower boxes down in time to dry for Matty and Zoe. I did *my* share before getting ready for my regular work because customers don't appreciate me wearing an apron with mud all down the front."

Matty ignored that dispute, focusing on Zoe to deliver a different argument. "Like Joyce wouldn't get dirty handling flats? Besides, you know the mix we're using, she doesn't. Go." She turned to Joyce. "You couldn't really have thought you could do this without getting dirty. Sit."

Zoe opened her mouth to protest again, but by now Matty, Rainie, and even Joyce were staring at her.

She got up and started off, muttering to Matt as she went by, "They're behind the clinic."

He caught up in two strides.

CHAPTER SIX

The last time a female had been this clear about not wanting to be in Matt's company, she'd been a bucking bronc not much short of a thousand pounds doing her best to unseat him.

Flowers sat in rows in the far reaches of the parking lot behind the medical clinic. No one else was there.

Zoe found three black plastic trays and started picking out plants.

"Look, Zoe, we got off on the wrong foot," he said to the back of her head. "Well, not that night in Cody."

Damn. Why had he brought that up?

"The other day. At Taylor's office, I mean." He'd thought her hands paused, but he must have imagined it.

He racked his brain for what to say next. And fell back on the familiar.

"Did you know my app—the one that started everything for me—started out for cowboys? Made it so I could put in all the variables and then it helped pick the rodeo that gave the best shot for the biggest purse with the lowest risk of time and expense. I didn't know much to start, but I kept reading and thinking and tinkering. The boys loved it.

"Talking with Harold Hopewell about it, he saw right off how it could apply to anybody. Now it lets people juggle all the factors of a trip—travel, hotel, eating expenses—so they see the whole package, not just the pieces. Plus you weight factors that mean the most to you. Say, you're somebody who doesn't mind long travel if it's to get to a great destination. Or you could decide easy travel, cushy hotel is more important than having a big adventure. That sort of thing."

He'd explained this often enough that he could say it in his sleep.

Apparently that was about the reaction it induced in her, too.

Picking out plants at full speed, she showed as much interest in what he'd said as if it had all been *blah, blah, blah.*

She separated the top tray—now full—from the other two, turned to him, and said two words:

"Hold this."

She returned to picking flowers as fast as she could.

He added a few more of the usual things he said about the app and his company. But then he found himself venturing into topics that weren't part of his usual interview fare.

"The thing with a new business is you have to keep investing in it to get it to grow. You start out with an idea and just yourself, but then you bring other people on board and they're counting on you to keep it going for the long-term. So you think differently and it all takes money. Most of the money coming in goes right back into the business. I was making more money rodeoing than I'm paying myself.

"Not complaining, because I'm building something. But people have this image and that's not what it's like."

She turned to him again. But only because she'd filled a second tray. "Hold this."

"Put it on top."

"No. The flowers will get smashed. Balance that one on your arm."

He maneuvered the first tray onto one forearm. She put the second on his other. They weren't heavy but being a flower loading dock was awkward.

And she'd sure made it so he couldn't touch her.

Not that he had any intention of touching her.

Only reason he was telling her this stuff was in hopes of smoothing things between them. Just so other people didn't notice and start talking.

Maybe also because he had been a jackass when she'd walked in to Taylor's office.

You. What are you doing here?

That's what had come out. What had been in his head was:

Her.

Here.

Now.

"It was that night."

She looked up at his abrupt words. "What?" Then seemed to regret it as she went back to the flowers.

"That night you and I … that was the night I met Harold Hopewell. The billionaire who invested to help me start my business. The thing about that is—"

"Busy night for you, because if I recall—though it's hazy after all this time—there wasn't much night left."

Yeah, she had a sharp edge to her tongue all right. He'd noticed she hadn't used it on the others.

"I went to a diner," he said evenly. "All-night place on the highway. Started talking to a guy who turned out to be the billionaire Harold Hopewell. Never would have known it to look at him. Or to talk to him."

"So running away from me is what got you your start in business."

"I didn't run—" Looking at her profile, he saw one raised eyebrow. It stopped the denial. He started again. "I left your bed—"

"*Your* bed. As you told me over and over. Since you owned the bed and breakfast and that was your usual room, which I was in only because they'd filled up and didn't know you were coming. You made that very clear. *Your* bed."

"*Our* bed," he snapped, then sucked in a breath, waited half a beat for her to argue more. She didn't. "I left our bed and went to the diner by the highway. And there was this guy sitting there and we started talking."

Sitting three stools away. The only other customer in the place. Even the guy behind the counter fell asleep. Talking about anything and everything other than why they were sitting there as dawn turned the artificial light into sickly paleness.

Only when people started filing in looking for breakfast did they move to the booth in the back corner.

That's when the talk had turned closer to home.

"He'd have liked you," he said now.

Harold *had* liked her. Well, what Matt had told him of her.

"There's time to go back, boy," Harold had said. "Spend more time with her, get to know her, see if there's any way one thing might lead to another. Because if you have a chance at the right kind of love, don't give that up for anything."

No, there hadn't been. No time. No way. No chance.

Not then. He'd known that from looking in that bathroom mirror.

And sure as hell not now. He knew that from looking at her face.

She picked up the final tray, now as full as the two he held.

"I wish *I'd* met Harold Hopewell so he could have donated the money we need for the telemedicine program."

She walked away from him, heading back toward the diner.

All was right with the world.

The flowers were planted. Knighton was beautified for the season. Matt Halderman was gone.

And Zoe was eating her third scoop of ice cream. But who was counting?

"Isn't that your third scoop?" Matty Brennan Currick asked from a seat on the library grounds, where the workers had gathered. The youngest Currick sat in her lap, sound asleep against her chest.

Zoe groaned.

Matty chuckled. "Come sit with me. I promise not to drool."

"Town looks great," Zoe said between spoonfuls of the ice cream Cal Ruskoff had arranged for the volunteers.

"Uh-huh," Matty said absently. "You know you're probably one of the smartest people I know, Zoe."

She had nothing to say to that. She made a noncommittal sound.

"You are," Matty said firmly. "On the other hand, I've been around longer than you have and one thing I've learned is that sometimes people come back into your life for a reason and—"

"Matty—"

"Just talking in generalities here. Not naming any names. But if *some-one* comes back into your life, you need to be on the lookout for there being a reason for it. You might think you've learned your lesson, moved on, gotten over. And then here comes that same lesson banging away at your heart and head with fists wearing spiked gloves. Metaphori-cally speaking, of course."

"Gee, that makes me feel better," Zoe said grimly.

"It's like doctors say about shots. This is going to hurt some but it's for your own good."

"Great. I'll be on the lookout, but really—"

"And then there's the switcheroo."

"Switcheroo?"

"Uh-huh. You're on the watch for the same lesson, but that does you no good, because eventually you realize it's the same person, but it's not the same lesson. You *have* moved on, you *have* gotten over that first lesson. But they're here to teach you another one this time."

"Matty, I don't know what you're thinking, but whatever it is, you're wrong. There's nothing… He… I mean, I don't—"

"He who?" she asked with wide, innocent eyes that not the most trusting soul would believe. "I'm talking about Dave and me."

Zoe settled for that noncommittal sound again. It was better than a groan.

"Or maybe," Matty stroked her hand over the soft hair of the sleep-ing child she and Dave had brought into the world, "you've both learned your major lessons—you know you *never* stop learning the smaller ones—and you're both here to stay. Together."

Matt came out of the old ranch house and sat on the side porch's top step in the predawn.

His favorite techie from his company had finished setting up his system about lunchtime the day before. To test it and to try to catch up after almost a week of limited access, Matt had worked straight through.

No problems. He'd even switched over to the backup system about four this morning to give that a workout. All good.

So Chris would leave this morning.

Odd that the thought gave Matt a twinge. He mostly preferred solitude. One reason he'd developed the app to start with was he'd chosen to go solo when he could afford it. Driving buddies would discuss—and argue about—the choices the app explored.

Frequently he'd put in long hours alone driving straight through to the next stop.

The way he'd done that night arriving in Cody at the bed and breakfast.

That night…

When he opened the door and saw Zoe.

"What the hell are you doing in my room?" he'd demanded.

She stood there in a towel. Two towels. But he wasn't paying much heed to the one around her head.

Steam from the bathroom backed her with a gauze curtain. Her skin glowed with the moisture, droplets blooming as patches of diamonds on the smooth ivory.

No clothes, no makeup, no fancy hair. Nothing but woman. So clean and fresh and honest.

He swallowed hard.

He'd been bone tired. No, deeper than bone. A tired that went right through the bone and into the marrow.

His mother had shown up at his previous rodeo. That hadn't been pretty.

Then, he'd gone out in an early round. Not even a sniff of the purse. That happened now and then to everybody. But it was happening more.

There weren't any old men riding broncs or bulls. He wasn't old. Not yet. But he wasn't young, either, not by rodeo standards. What was he going to do when he was done?

He'd driven longer and farther than he'd planned to try to stay ahead of that question. Pulling up to where he knew he always had a room. This room.

Because he owned the place.

He hadn't wanted to bother the managers, who'd be up at dawn preparing breakfasts. So he went up the back way, swung the door open and there she was.

Like nothing he'd ever seen before.

"What the hell are you doing in *my* room?" she'd demanded back. Then she'd added, "Close the door, you're letting all the warm air out, Matt Halderman."

He'd squinted at her, trying to make the mists of steam and memory part to reveal an answer. She knew him? She couldn't. Because he couldn't have known her and forgotten her. Not this one. Not possible.

"Zoe Parisi." She held out a hand.

He looked to see if the towel held. So sue him.

It held. One edge tucked tightly into the top that came under her armpits and allowed only the first swell of the breasts below it to show. Her shoulders were bare, except for those diamond droplets. Her neck long and elegant. Her face a pure oval under the turban. And her eyes…

He took her hand. It was slender. The nails short, unpolished. Yet strength in her handshake.

Automatically, he started, "Matt Halder—"

"Halderman. I know." She took her hand back, moved to one side. The towel came to just above her knees—why did they have such damned large towels?—showing pale legs and bare feet as slender and strong as her hands. "I just said so. Didn't you hear me?"

"But—?"

"I'm Hugh and Ruth Moski's granddaughter."

That flickered a memory, though it was hard to snag with those bare shoulders and that towel just above her breasts. And her eyes. And her mouth. But especially her eyes. And that surprised him, because he'd always focused on breasts and legs.

"From Knighton," he said abruptly, the memory coming to his tongue before it fully bloomed in a mind otherwise occupied. "Knighton, Wyoming."

"That's right. Now that that's settled. What are we going to do about this room situation?"

CHAPTER SEVEN

Zoe hadn't been sleeping well these past days.

She would not think about why. Especially not now, while she was standing outside the clinic in front of many of the citizens of Lewis and Clark counties to unveil the fundraising thermometer tracking progress toward the amount needed to join the telemedicine program.

Doc Johnson pulled the bed sheet off the large cardboard thermometer to applause.

They'd purposely waited until they had some money to provide the psychological boost of having a base filled in.

"And another piece of great news! We have a foundation that's agreed to match our donations dollar for dollar this year."

"Thank you, Cal," somebody called from the audience.

He held up a protesting hand. "Not me. Just brought it to the attention of folks interested in projects like this."

Zoe pointed out, "This matching grant means we only have to raise *half* the money if we do it this year compared to what we'd need if we wait until next year."

"Talk about inflation," someone murmured.

"Talk about a great opportunity." That came out strongly, but Zoe could feel her voice weakening.

"What about ongoing costs?"

"There are some, but modest. Joining the program is the big expense because of all the set-up costs."

"What do you think, Doc?" someone asked from the back. Then added, "Doc Johnson."

"I think this is exactly the reason Knighton needs Dr. Parisi. To bring in great ideas and knowledge to benefit the medical care of every one of us. She's pulled me right into this century, whether I like it or not." That drew chuckles. "And I like it!" Most applauded that. "Just last week I had a teleconference with specialists at the university that helped with a case. And I was able to help a young doctor at a clinic in Sweetwater. But those are one-time special events. This program we're trying to get in now would make that an everyday occurrence if need be. This program will make a difference for you if you come into the clinic or if you are so sick you can't leave home."

"Like me being sick this winter?" Earl asked.

Zoe beamed at him. "Exactly."

"That's right," Doc Johnson said. "Though, if he'd called in when he was first feeling bad it might not have gone on as long as it did."

"Pneumonia," Earl said to those around him.

She wouldn't have shared the diagnosis, but if he wanted to, fine. "Once we knew what it was, I could have monitored him by video-conferencing. That would have meant fewer trips here for Earl and fewer trips up to his place for me. Both those are good for the patient. I'm sure you can all see why fewer trips to the clinic are good," she said wryly.

That drew a good-natured rumbling of agreement.

"Even better is that more of you will be spared trips to Cheyenne or Billings or Denver or beyond to see a specialist, because we can do the consultation here—you, your hometown doctor, and the specialist, all together."

She cleared her throat and Matty handed her a bottle of water.

"For those of you who don't know, Dr. Parisi's researched this thoroughly," Matty said, giving her time to drink. "If you have any questions, there's a whole binder of information—one here at the clinic and one at the library—that anyone can look through."

Zoe nodded her thanks to Matty and continued, "Another major benefit of the program is if I can see a patient by video, I'm spending less time driving so I can be here at the clinic seeing more patients along with Doc Johnson. That means all of you can get an appointment sooner *and* spend less time waiting."

"That sounds real good, Doc Z, but what makes you think an old coot like Earl could learn how to do this?" someone in the middle asked.

"Hey, if it's Doc Z's smiling face on the screen I'll learn how," Earl said.

That drew chuckles and laughter.

"We'll have training sessions," she said. "We'll set up a roster of volunteers to go help at the homes of folks who aren't sure how to do it."

"I can organize the volunteers for that," offered Val Trimarco.

"Unless it's when the baby's coming," said her husband-to-be, once again with Addie in his arms.

"Thank you, Val. And don't worry, Jack. It'll be either this July—if we can raise the money fast—or next July. But it would be so much better if we could do it *this* year."

She took another drink. Her voice was definitely going.

"That's right," Matty picked up, "we want to get this program started this year to benefit everybody and to take full advantage of the matching grant. So be generous with your donations. Let's fill in this thermometer so fast it'll look like we're all spiking a fever."

That drew chuckles as Dave Currick and Cal Ruskoff moved through the crowd with their hats upended as receptacles for cash. Their wives accompanied them, writing out receipts.

Matty kept up the encouragement as she went. "This is a great opportunity. Anybody who ends up having to take a run to Cheyenne or Denver to go to a specialist in the next twelve months would sure regret not putting in more money now. We all put in some and we'll all end up saving, not to mention giving Zoe more time for actual doctoring like she mentioned."

Matty was so much better at this than she was. Thank heavens she was here.

A few more minutes and she could slip back through the clinic and pick up her message slips from Polly.

The clinic manager believed in technology, but she also believed in backup systems for the backup systems. So she took notes from callers directly into the computer system, but also wrote the headline on a message slip. Zoe loved it because it let her triage the slips.

Maybe she'd go to the apartment she rented from her grandparents, make the necessary callbacks, then take a nap … until next week.

Matt had hung back, watching and listening.

When it seemed to be winding down, he retreated, unseen, and went into the drug store for the items he'd come to town for. Since he'd stopped rodeoing regularly, his first aid kit had dwindled to a couple bandages and an end piece of tape. That did fine for working on a computer, not so good for ranch work. On top of that, his muscles were no longer accustomed to this kind of labor.

He wasn't sure if he'd avoided the gathering in front of the clinic because he didn't want to be called out for not just paying for the whole thing. Or, more generally, he wasn't ready to become reacquainted with Knighton en masse.

His purchases completed, he was exiting by the door that led to the side street when it hit him that there was another question—why had he watched and listened at all? He could have gone right into the drugstore, made his purchases, and been gone nearly an hour ago.

Surely he hadn't lingered because he wanted to see—

Zoe.

Coming out the side door of the clinic just across the street from him.

He watched as she spotted him, then decided to pretend she hadn't.

She headed down her sidewalk, away from Main Street.

He crossed the street and caught up with her.

"Hi, Zoe. Nice speech."

Though there'd been something in it that had bothered him. Darned if he could remember what it was now. Had to be because he had a lot on his mind. Not because she was here in front of him, giving him that cool-eyed survey so unlike that night…

"Too bad it didn't make you want to donate."

That snapped him out of reminiscing. "Ah, that's right, because all you want from me is money."

"Exactly. And I'm tired right now. So, if you don't mind…"

"But I do. Mind. I've got something to say."

"Say it." She tipped her chin down, while her eyes came up, looking at him at a slant. It was a lot like a certain memorable saddle bronc used to look. An expression that said clear as day, "What darned fool thing do you think you're going to try now, mister?"

"You look tired. Are you getting sick?"

She took a step away. "If that's all you have to say—"

"You wouldn't really have wanted me to stick around that night." That stopped her. "I was a rodeo cowboy. Up one minute, flat the next. On the road all the time. And you … you were a kid, really just a kid. You had all that schooling to become a doctor ahead of you. And you did it. You—"

"Oh, I'm fully prepared to concede that you did me a favor, Matt."

"Okay," he said slowly. Somehow having her agree didn't feel as good as he'd have expected. "Well, then, what do you want me to say?"

"Not a thing. I don't want you to say a thing except that you're donating to our fund."

He pulled back. "It's not like my business has money stacked up in a back room ready to hand out to whoever wants it."

And what money he had was earmarked for other goals.

Her eyes narrowed. "You have enough to run a hospice for horses. I know the money for the land's been spent, but you must have more put aside. Funds for operating."

"That's for the horses."

"*People* need it."

"It's a good cause, I'm not arguing that. Glad to give a donation, but—"

"Glad to get a donation." She held out her hand.

He pulled out his wallet, shifted the drug store bag to the crook of his elbow to free both hands so he could open the wallet, and withdrew all the folding money from it.

She stared at the bills in his hand. "Do you expect me to be touched that you're offering to empty your wallet when you could write a check to cover the whole thing?"

"Don't expect anything except that you take the donation if you want it. Do you?"

"Hell, yes." She took the money from his fingers, then marched off.

He stayed put.

Which was saying something, considering the urge to go after her.

Three days later, he flipped through the mail he'd retrieved from his box.

An envelope with the clinic's return address caught his attention. He ripped it open.

A single sheet provided him an official receipt for a donation of $157.

CHAPTER EIGHT

Zoe and her grandmother walked into the diner together for lunch.

They tried to do this several times a week. Too often, Zoe's schedule interfered. Once in a while Ruth let running Dave Currick's law office get in the way, though she had things so well organized it usually wasn't an issue.

Zoe stopped dead a few paces in, as soon as her eyes took in the strange sight before her.

Mostly empty stools.

The only two that were occupied did not hold any of the group of men—including her grandfather—who were here so frequently they were called the Stool Sitters by one and all.

At one end of the counter, a tall, rangy stranger dressed in working cowboy attire that appeared well-used and well-cared-for was ordering takeout from Rainie.

In the middle sat Joyce Aberdick, apparently on her lunch break from the bank.

"Where are the Stool Sitters?" Zoe asked.

"That outdoors and camping outlet over in Jefferson's having its semiannual going out of business sale today," Rainie said. "The whole lot of them went. Not that any of them do any camping and not much outdoors because they're always here cluttering up my counter."

"Be prepared to get a canteen for your birthday, Zoe," Ruth warned. She headed toward their usual booth. "I've told your grandfather that if he ever gives me another item from that place I'm having the locks changed, not only on the house, but the garage, too, and that got his attention."

"Grandma, let's sit at the counter. We never get to—just for a change."

Ruth shrugged and altered course to the open end of the counter.

Zoe soon regretted her impulse and her grandmother's indulgence, as Joyce held forth loudly enough that there was no private conversation to be had.

After ordering, Zoe acknowledged her error with a slight eye roll that only Ruth could see. She received a faint, philosophical shrug in return.

They heard in great detail how crops were doing, how Brandy from the post office had cried over a new haircut, how construction was going on the latest addition at the Curricks' Slash-C Ranch, how Cal Ruskoff had won the bidding for a bull at a recent auction, how Taylor had brought their kids to a legal hearing in Jefferson and how the opposing lawyer had objected, but the judge ended up giving them books he kept for his grandchildren. And on and on. Zoe thought her brain cells had all been anesthetized.

Until Joyce uttered the name Matt Halderman.

"Nobody can quite tell what he's doing out there. You know he calls it Pegasus Ranch, even though it's just a corner of the H Bar H that was in the Halderman family forever. Connor Malloy bought some of the Pratcher Place so he has about the same number of acres, but—"

"Really, Joyce?" Rainie asked. "You're going to talk about acreage instead of Matt Halderman?"

Joyce giggled. "Oh, I know. When he came to the Beautify Knighton Day, he *did*. My, oh my, he definitely did beautify Knighton. He's *so* handsome."

Behind the counter, Rainie pursed her mouth.

"Wouldn't say handsome, precisely. Even before his nose got a bit rearranged by a bull or a bronc or a jealous husband, he wasn't precisely handsome. For one thing, his face isn't symmetrical," the waitress said, with the air of one accustomed to spotting flaws in super models.

And that was hooey, Zoe thought. He was, too, handsome. That was part of the problem.

His problem, she meant.

She didn't have a problem with how he looked. Not anymore. So it wouldn't matter how much Joyce gushed over him.

Only the next gush wasn't Joyce's, it was Rainie's. Apparently she'd just gone in for a dramatic pause. "Nope, not exactly handsome, but he sure is *sexy*."

Joyce moaned. "*So* sexy."

"For heaven sakes, act your age, woman," Ruth said.

Joyce colored, but Rainie said, "It's a little harmless fun. Just looking is all. He's even younger than Shane Garrison, that New York detective Lisa Currick married," she added in an aside to Zoe, as if Zoe didn't already know it, "and he's the one who set my heart to pitter-pattering ... if only I didn't have the kids and George."

Ruth snorted. "As if Shane could see any other woman alive besides Lisa."

"Yeah, that was another little obstacle we would've had to get over. From what I saw the other day, seems like it might be a similar situation with Matt Halderman."

Slowly—slow enough that Zoe could see what was coming yet could do nothing to stop or change it, just like being in a car accident—Rainie turned and looked down the counter at her.

Joyce's gaze followed the same course.

More slowly, her grandmother's did, too.

Good heavens, even the stranger waiting for his order looked at her.

She wanted to drop her head to the counter. She wanted to hide under the stool. She wanted to run.

But the basic rule of medicine also applied here—first, do no harm.

Dropping her head, hiding, or running would do a world of harm.

"Order up!" the cook called from in back.

Zoe raised her brows and looked back at the three women. The stranger could just mind his own business.

"You think I know anything about who Matt Halderman might be dating? I don't. All I know—"

"Who he's dating. That's good," Rainie said with a chuckle and a swipe at the counter.

"—is he said no when I asked for a donation to get us in the tele-medicine program." She wanted to stop there. She really wanted to stop there, but fairness made her add, "Well, he said his business wouldn't donate. He made a personal one." With each word she saw their suspicion deepening.

"Rainie, I think you're right," Joyce said in a tone of having discovered a cheap cure for the cold. "Why the way he looked at Zoe, you—"

"Especially when her back was turned," Rainie said.

"—could practically hear the sizzle. Didn't you two date when you were younger?" she asked avidly.

"No." They all looked at her—yes, the stranger, too—clearly expecting, demanding more. "We never dated."

She wished she could take those words back and smooth them out. Make them sound easy and amused. Too late.

"Well, there's *something*," Joyce said.

"Rainie! Order up!" the cook yelled.

The waitress waved him off, focusing on Zoe. "He's clearly smitten with you."

"Apparently not," she said as coolly as she could. "Since you'd think a man who was smitten would donate toward a program that—"

"*Something* must have happened between you," Joyce said with absolute assurance. "I sensed it before. The way you two interact is different."

Zoe tried a light laugh. "Just because I don't fall at the guy's feet…"

"Like any normal woman would," Rainie inserted.

"Rainie!" The cook stuck his arm through the pass-through and shook the oversized takeout bag.

"All right, all right." She took the bag and headed toward the stranger.

"So I'm right! Something did happen. There's a *past*, a *history* there." Joyce Aberdick could make a full-blown conspiracy theorist sound like a skeptic. "I *knew* it."

Zoe tried to curb her exasperation. The woman had *known* it for all of about two minutes. Before Rainie's comments she'd had no clue.

But the exasperation was also self-directed.

First Matty Currick and now these women? Did she wear a darned billboard?

Joyce sighed delightedly. "It feels just like one of those movies where the man's done the woman wrong but they're *soul mates* and the woman just *knows* it—"

"Oh, for heaven sakes, Joyce."

"—so she doesn't let him push her away—"

"Or push her down the stairs," Zoe said, "or punch her in the face or stab her with a metal pipe or—"

"Good Lord," Ruth said under her breath.

"Sorry, Grandma. ER experience."

"—and just keeps loving him," Joyce continued, undeterred by Zoe's dose of reality. "Keeps loving him and loving him, no matter what he does until he just breaks down and cries at how *wonderful* she is. And—"

"That is not only unrealistic, Joyce. It's dangerous. Do you know how many women—?"

"—it's so *romantic*. If Matt broke your heart—"

"You're making all this up, Joyce. Every. Single. Bit."

"—you've got to forgive him."

Now her discomfort had her imagining the stranger was dragging his feet leaving after settling up with Rainie.

"Matt Halderman doesn't need or want my forgiveness." *You wouldn't really have wanted me to stick around that night.* "Far from it. Except for declining to have his business donate to a project that would help every person in Lewis and Clark counties, he—"

"But—"

"Joyce Aberdick," Ruth interrupted. Zoe had been fully aware that Ruth had said little through this discussion. That might be bad. Very bad. "I will say two things to you.

"First, if any man treated my granddaughter the way you describe those men doing I'd despair of her most basic commonsense if she did what you say these women do. Second, your thinking that's romantic makes me despair for *your* most basic commonsense and makes me doubt I should have my money in the institution you're associated with."

Joyce's cheeks flamed.

"But, Ruth, they're so popular. Especially with the young girls and—"

"Popular." Ruth made it a curse word. "If that's so, their parents need to deliver a good talking-to to those girls, before they go off with the first abuser they encounter. Brainless. Now, I have a third thing to say to you. You're late returning to your desk from lunch."

Joyce gasped and clasped her hands to her chest, eyes starting as she turned to the clock that confirmed the dire news.

CHAPTER NINE

On the sidewalk after lunch, Zoe gave her grandmother's cheek a quick kiss.

"See you later."

"Zoe Theresa."

Zoe stopped in mid-escape, and turned back to Ruth.

"Those things you said in there. Has any man ever treated you—?"

"No. No, really, Grand." She rarely used that childhood nickname anymore, but it slipped out now.

"Your stepfather—"

"No. Never to me or the other kids. He slapped Mom twice I know of, but his forte was verbal abuse. But I've seen all those injuries and worse in ERs and clinics and safe houses. I wasn't lying or exaggerating. That's why it's so dangerous—"

"I never thought you were exaggerating and certainly not lying. And I agree it's dangerous."

"Oh."

"What happened, Zoe?"

"I don't—"

"When you came back from that wilderness medical training the summer before you started medical school, something had happened. Was it during the training?"

"What? No. The training was great. I learned so much and—"

"Then what?"

"Nothing, Grandma. Really. Just growing pains, I suppose." She kissed that familiar, much-loved cheek again. "Gotta go."

Matt stood beside Walker Riley looking through the fence of the near corral at the horses they'd just unloaded from the trailer Walker had hauled here.

He'd stood next to Walker many a time looking at rodeo stock. Early on soaking up every word of knowledge and insight the older man cared to share. Eventually as equals—or pretty near—exchanging observations and opinions.

"Kalli's got that song about where love lives in your head," Walker said, referring to his wife.

Matt was about to deny it when he realized he'd been humming the tune. "It's catchy."

"She also thinks it's important for you to think about."

"No need. I got my answer and I'm working on making it happen."

Walker gave a short sigh, not needing to say that his wife didn't agree and that between his wife and his friend his vote went to his wife.

Matt got all that. Hell, he trusted Kalli's judgment most times. Just not this time.

He changed the subject. "What do you think of the setup so far?"

"So far?"

Matt ignored the sharpened point of that question. "What you've seen," he said, without looking at his friend.

"It's got potential. Lot of work ahead of you on the place, but that's never bothered you. You got a couple real troublemakers in that herd, but you know that, too. As for what I hauled in? They look rough and the trailer's worse. You should have heard Gulch holding forth on its condition."

Gulch Miller had been wrapping up his rodeo career when Walker began his. Matt didn't know how it started—maybe they didn't either— but there was a tie between the two men that had extended to Kalli, the kids as they came along, and even to Matt when Walker had taken him under his wing. Gulch was definitely part of the Riley family. An outspoken one.

"If there'd been time," Walker continued, "I'd've cleaned it out before the trip, because—"

"Hey, I appreciate you doing this, jumping in last minute like you did."

"No problem."

"It would've been a problem if you hadn't come through. And then picking up lunch at the diner on your way in. Hard to find help that'll go the extra mile to pick up food."

Walker gave a half grin. "After you said you hadn't gotten around to the comforts yet, I wasn't running the risk that included food."

"I suppose that's why Kalli sent that cooler's worth, too."

"Yup."

"Well, it's not quite that bad. I do have the basics, including food."

"As good as that lunch we had from the diner?"

"Nope. And not half as good as what Kalli makes, so thank you."

"No problem. I should get going. But there was something from when I stopped in town that I wanted to ask you about."

"In town?" He snorted. "What? Does Zoe Parisi have a Wanted poster up on me? A bull's-eye with my face in the center? A petition against letting me drink the same water as the good people of Lewis and Clark counties?"

In the silence that followed his words echoed.

"Zoe Parisi?" Walker asked mildly.

"Never mind."

"This Zoe about yay high?" He held up a level hand. "Dark blue eyes, long hair, nothing fussy about her?"

"Sounds like her." So why did he want to argue with that description? Want to declare it didn't half capture her. "What did she say?"

"Not a whole lot. Though it sounds like she's had some tough experiences. You wouldn't... This bull's-eye with your face in the center wouldn't have anything to do with something physical, would it?"

"Physical..." *Slim legs wrapped around him, hands stroking his face, his back, body welcoming him, drawing him in...* His head jerked up. "You mean *hit* her? She wasn't saying that. She wouldn't—"

"No, she wasn't." Walker said firmly. "But… I didn't get all of it. It was mostly other folks talking. The waitress."

"Rainie."

"An older woman with your Zoe."

"Her grandmother. Ruth Moski. But Zoe's not mi—" Too late.

"And a woman in between Rainie and Ruth. Talked a lot. A lot. And there was something about a bank—"

"Joyce. Joyce Aberdick."

"Yeah, well, she was on at Zoe about how she should forgive you everything. Or maybe it was *anything*. I never expected to know all your conquests, but this seemed … different."

"It's not. Not a conquest. Not different. It's nothing. So there's no need to be telling Kalli. She'll be back on me about how I've got this all wrong and that song."

"I won't tell Kalli if you don't want me to, even though…" Matt gave him a look and Walker raised his hands in surrender. "But is there something between you and this Zoe?"

"Why would there be?"

Walker gave him a sideways look, clearly recognizing the evasion. "Well, if you need to be forgiven… And that seemed to be the trend of the conversation. Plus, she didn't seem particularly happy about the others associating you with her or—"

"Hi."

They looked around at the unexpected voice.

A kid. Maybe ten, eleven, with a rusty colored, flop-eared dog as his heels, stood between them and the barn.

"Hi," Matt said back with enthusiasm.

Okay, yeah, he was relieved at the interruption. And of all the potential eavesdroppers around here a kid like this would be his second choice. His first choice would be the Widow Brontman, who was mostly deaf.

No, on second thought, she read lips, moving this kid to number one.

"We're neighbors, so I wanted to introduce myself."

About a dozen things hit Matt at once. The first was that if they were neighbors the kid must be from the home ranch of the H Bar H. *His* ranch … what used to be his family's ranch.

The second was that he could be looking at himself twenty years ago.

The third was that the kid was on his dignity, acting as grown up as he could.

The rest of the dozen he wouldn't bother with.

"Matt Halderman." He tugged off one work glove and extended a hand that was dirty despite the glove.

In return, the kid presented a hand that made his look pristine. They shook.

"Jarrod Malloy, Mr. Halderman, sir. And this is Midnight." The dog's ears flicked at his name.

Mr. Halderman? Sir?

Matt felt as if he'd been poked in the gut. "Matt," he got out.

"And I'm Walker Riley." His friend was hiding a laugh as he shook hands with the boy.

Showed how young the kid was that he didn't react to that name. Even those who didn't follow rodeo closely had heard of Walker Riley.

"Midnight's an interesting name for this fella," Walker said, scratching behind the dog's ears.

"He's Midnight because that's when he was born and it was the first time I ever got to stay up that late. 'Course that was years ago."

Walker nodded his understanding that the kid was now a man of the world who routinely stayed up until the small hours.

"Well, it's been a pleasure meeting you and Midnight, but it's time for me to head out." He tugged the brim of his hat to the boy, then extended a hand to Matt. They shook strongly. "We'll be in touch about when Kalli and the kids and I can come. Probably a Sunday and we'll plan to stay overnight if that's all right."

"As long as you can stay. I know it's tough during rodeo season. Tell them I said hey."

"Will do."

As his truck pulled out he waved back through the open window.

For an instant, Matt felt an emptiness. Walker, Kalli, their kids, and Gulch were the closest he'd had to true family for a long time. Yeah, his mother was alive, but—

"Need some help?" the kid asked hopefully. "What are you doing? You've got a lot of horses. What're you going to do with them? Breeding?"

Matt turned and looked at the trio in the near corral. "Would you breed them?"

"No way, but my dad says you gotta respect different strokes for different folks."

Matt laughed. "Your dad's a wise man and you're not a bad judge of horseflesh. I'll tell you, Jarrod, what you've stumbled on here is a sort of retirement home for horses. A brand new retirement home. Those three are the latest arrivals. So what's up next for me is mucking out the trailer. That's not exactly the most fun you can have—"

"That's okay. I can help."

"—but if you're willing, I'd be happy of the help. Only—"

"Sure thing."

"—do your folks know where you are? Is it okay with them?"

"This used to be part of our place, so it's practically the same as staying on our place." Their eyes met. The boy's gave in. "I'll text Dad. Mom's off in Denver again."

While Matt moved the two wheelbarrows in place to receive the bedding from the trailer, Jarrod peppered him with questions at the same time his thumbs flew over the face of his phone with a dexterity known only to the young, limber, and never injured.

Jarrod was thrilled to discover the horses were rodeo alums, especially bucking broncs. "Were you in the rodeo, too?"

"Yup. For a while. Then I started a business."

"Oh. A business. But rodeo's cool—Dad says okay!" he announced after a flurry of thumb riffs.

"Must've said more than that with all that tapping."

"Well, first he asked if I'd done my chores. And I had. And then he said not to bother you. And I told him I'm not. And then he said not to talk your ear off. And I said I wasn't."

"Okay, let's get to work."

Matt went deeper into the trailer. The kid was a good worker and they got a rhythm going with Matt pulling the bedding material from the front of the trailer toward the back, where Jarrod pushed it over the edge into the wheelbarrows.

All the while, the kid talked. About Midnight, about the ranch, about school, about baseball, about his friends, about horses.

Matt emptied both barrows and returned inside, reaching up to pull out the mess where some fool had packed hay in an upper compartment. It wasn't easy. Partly because of the angle of raising his arms to reach the corners, partly because pulling it out meant most of it landed on him, partly because he had to keep reminding himself not to swear out loud with the kid nearby.

So when the kid's talk switched to questions, he answered with only part of his mind.

"You used to live in my house?"

That question did catch his attention.

"Yep."

And now that he was more aware, he realized the kid was coughing. Had been for a while.

"What was it like back when you were a kid?"

"Pretty much the same. The mountains don't move much."

The kid chuckled and that became a cough, too. And he sounded out of breath. Sure they'd been working, but that hard?

And then Matt turned and caught sight of the dog standing at alert outside the trailer, focused on the boy, and Matt would swear there was a frown tucked between its eyebrows.

"What's the matter?" he asked the kid.

"I'm okay," Jarrod said in a small voice.

Matt put down his rake and went to the boy. "You don't sound okay. What's the matter?"

"My... uh, my chest feels tight."

Heart attack? A kid his age? "Do you, um, have heart trouble?"

"No." But his breathing wasn't the best. He coughed again. "Used to have asthma."

"Used to? Sounds like you have it now. Don't you have something for that? Meds?" There was something specific—

"Haven't had it for … ages."

"Okay, I believe you, but you need something now, right? C'mon out of here so I can see you."

He stepped down, looped an arm around the kid's waist and brought him to the barn floor, too.

Inhaler. That was the name of it.

"Where's your inhaler, Jarrod?"

"Left it home."

Matt swore a blue streak in his head. But that didn't slow him from grabbing his phone and hitting a number.

CHAPTER TEN

"Matty, I need Zoe Parisi's number."

"Oh, do you? Well, I'm not sure she—"

"Professionally. I need a doctor. Now."

She rattled off the number without a moment's hesitation. "She's at Taylor and Cal's right now. Is there anything I can do?"

"If there is, I'll call."

He hit the numbers Matty had given him.

She answered with "Dr. Parisi." He'd never heard anything so wonderful in his life.

"Zoe. It's Matt Halderman. Jarrod Malloy—a kid about ten—"

"I know him."

"He's here with me at Pegasus Ranch. He says his chest feels tight. He says he used to have asthma. He doesn't have his meds."

"Does he have an emergency inhaler at home?"

He repeated the question to Jarrod, who nodded. "Yes," Matt told Zoe.

Through the phone he could hear Zoe moving. Thought he caught the sound of a heavy-duty zipper. "Are his lips blue?"

"No." The swearing went off in his head again. Blue lips couldn't be good. If that was next—

"Are his fingernails blue?"

Matt picked up one of the boy's hands. The one he wasn't using to cover his mouth as he coughed.

"No."

"Is he coughing?"

"Yes. A lot."

"His breathing—?"

"More like wheezing."

"Okay, load him in your truck. Make sure he's sitting up and stays sitting up. Keep the windows up but don't turn on the AC. If you have any hot coffee handy get him to sip it, but don't take time to make any. A cup is good. Not much more. Head to his house. Right now. I might meet you on the way. If not I'll see you at the house. Questions?"

"Should I call 911?" He hadn't right off because he knew how long it could take emergency vehicles to get to rural areas.

"This will be a lot faster. Anything else?"

"No."

"Go." She clicked off.

"Get in the truck. Front seat," he told Jarrod.

If the kid started to pass out, he could keep him upright with one arm and drive with the other. Matt sprinted back into the barn, grabbed the thermos, and was in the driver's seat before Jarrod was done buckling in.

The dog was starting to climb in the front seat, too.

"In the back," Matt said.

"Please. Can't. He."

"Fine. On the floor then." The dog seemed to understand, sliding into the foot well, under Jarrod's boots. Matt handed over the thermos. "Here."

Matt turned the truck around, making sure all the windows were up, just before spewing dust as he turned toward the main house.

"Sorry," the kid said.

"Forget sorry. You've got three jobs now—keep breathing nice and easy, keep sitting up, and sip some of that coffee. Small sips, also nice and easy."

From the corner of his eye he saw the kid open the thermos and pour out about a third of a cup. He made a face at the first sip.

"Too bad," Matt said. "Sip away, tough guy."

Jarrod gave a small grin.

"Thought of a fourth job. Do you know of a faster way to your house than this main road?" Maybe things had changed. He'd been gone a long time. A new road could have been put in—

"Not in a truck."

He understood. There were routes a horse could take that were so much more direct that even at an easy pace a rider could arrive before a truck. "Refill that cup and keep sipping."

"People like this stuff?"

Matt didn't know if it was his imagination, but he thought the kid's breathing sounded better. Easier, quieter.

"Can't get by without it."

He accelerated through a straight patch of decent road, but had to brake as the road dipped down and curved to cross another branch of the old creek bed that had been dry as long as he could remember. He came out of it accelerating again. Finally, they crested the last hill, saw the house on the horizon.

The only house he'd ever thought of as home.

Fir trees his dad had planted to the northwest had jumped up since he'd last seen them. And someone had planted trees on the other side of the long, low house.

The porch was still there. Stretching from one end of the house to the other, with the broad opening where the steps came up to the double front doors.

But his focus left the past because there, closer than the house, was a vehicle coming toward them.

As they neared, the other vehicle stopped. Zoe got out, grabbed a bag from the seat behind her and was on Jarrod's side of the road when Matt braked to a hard stop.

She had the door open immediately.

"Hey, there, Jarrod and Midnight," she said, easy and relaxed. She pulled on medical gloves then scooched next to the boy. She put a stethoscope to his chest while her eyes went over his face. "Lean forward a bit."

Quickly, she scooped up the back of the kid's t-shirt and placed the stethoscope there, her focus totally on what she was hearing as she checked several places.

She removed the stethoscope from her ears and let it drop around her neck as she eased Jarrod to sit back. She lifted each eyelid for a second.

The dog didn't move other than its eyes and ears, taking in every word, every touch.

"I'm feeling better, Dr. Z," Jarrod said.

"Good to hear. You'll feel even better after this."

Matt heard that zipper sound again and realized it was Velcro opening on the bag now resting on the pickup's threshold.

"You haven't done this for a while, so we're going to use a spacer."

She shook what Matt recognized as an inhaler, took caps off it and a plastic tube. She fit the inhaler into the tube. She handed it to Jarrod with the open end of the tube toward him.

"First, breathe out. Easy," she instructed. "Good. Spacer between your teeth, now close your lips. No looking down. Keep that chin up. Breathe in through your mouth, slow. Just like that. Pull it in as deep as you can."

She had a hand on the boy's back and Matt suspected she could feel that breath coming in.

"You're doing great, Jarrod. Take it out and hold your breath. Let's see if you can hold it while Matt counts to ten."

After half a second of surprise, he started counting down from ten.

At one, Zoe said, "Good going. Now slowly let that breath out of your mouth. Good… good… That was excellent, Jarrod. Though you did get a break on that countdown. Who knew Matt could count that fast?"

"Hey, I wasn't expecting New Year's Eve out here on the range. Still looking around for the big ball coming down and all the people."

She never looked away from the boy. "Well, we're going to have more people—not Times Square kind of people, but a few more—pretty soon. Because I called your folks on my way over here. Let's take another listen."

"Mom's out of town. Again."

She used the stethoscope front and back. "Uh-huh. Tell me how you're doing now."

"Better. Really."

She nodded. "Can you tell me what you were doing when this started?"

"Helping Matt clean out a trailer that his new horses came in. I wanted to help and he said I could do that."

"That's good reporting, Jarrod. And the fact that you could talk that much without coughing's a good sign."

He grinned and she grinned back.

Matt felt a jolt like he'd taken a time or two on a bronc.

Delayed reaction to worry about the kid. Had to be.

"So, let me get packed up here," she said, "then we can drive up to the house at a slow, steady pace like they use for the queen in England. Not like Matt was doing heading up the hill. And then we'll check you out again."

Matt could have left.

Zoe was there. The boy's father was there. And they had him resting now after a change of clothes and another go-round with the inhaler in the kid's room.

Jarrod's room…

Did the kid have the same room he'd had growing up?

That would be weird.

It had been weird enough sitting on a strange couch set in the wrong place in the living room.

Other things had been changed, too. Looked like the kitchen had been redone. The rock fireplace hadn't been touched. That was good.

When he started itemizing more changes, he decided it was time to move from the living room to the porch.

Zoe came out in mid-conversation with Connor Malloy.

"—and certainly no sign of infection, though we'll keep an eye on him a few days. With how fast he's bounced back it's likely an allergic reaction to a new irritant."

"He's been so good for so long, it doesn't figure. What new irritant could it be? I swear he's been over every square inch of our place," Connor said.

"I'd recommend you go down with Matt and take a look…"

She let it die out as Connor shook his head. "Cherie can't get here until tomorrow at the earliest and I'm not leaving him. Would you mind going, Zoe? You'd probably recognize what might have done it before I would. If we don't pin down what triggered this, I might not let him out of my sight."

"Just don't let him get out of the house without the inhaler," she said.

"No way that'll happen again. But would you check, Zoe? I know it's your day off and—"

"Okay."

"Thanks. Thanks a lot. And thanks to you, Matt. Should've said it earlier." He stuck his hand out. "I'm real grateful for what you did to help Jarrod."

He met the man's hand. "I'm sorrier than I can say if something at my place caused this. Can I… uh, I'd like to say good-bye if it's okay."

"Sure, c'mon."

"Keep it short," Zoe ordered.

"I will."

She followed them in the house and down the hall, probably to make sure Matt lived up to his promise.

Jarrod wasn't in his old room. He was in the one they'd used as a guest room. He'd caught a glimpse through the open door of his old room. An office now.

"*Matt.*" Jarrod dropped the book he'd been reading and sat up fast. He shot a look toward his father. "I mean Mr. Halderman, sir."

"Matt's fine." He patted Midnight, who'd stepped forward with a wagging tail. "How're you feeling?"

"Good. The worst part was that coffee you made me drink." He screwed up his face and they all chuckled.

"Guess I don't have to worry about you sneaking my coffee for a while," Connor said.

"No way. In fact, I feel all better, so I can go back with you and—"

"Whoa." Matt's hand on his shoulder stopped him from swinging his legs off the bed. "Rest easy there. I've pledged us both to take it easy if I came back to see you. Just to say good-bye."

"Bye? Bye for today? Or... This doesn't mean I can't go back to Pegasus Ranch, does it, because really, really I feel fine."

"That depends," Connor said. "Dr. Parisi is going back with Matt to take a look and see if they can figure out what caused this."

"That's right," she said with that warm, calming smile to the boy. "You've been doing just fine with hay and horses and everything else on a ranch, so it's likely something very specific." She tipped her head, still looking at the boy. "Think you might be allergic to Matt?"

The kid laughed.

No, only Zoe Parisi was allergic to Matt Halderman.

CHAPTER ELEVEN

She pulled up next to his truck outside the Pegasus Ranch barn, parked, then went around to the front passenger door of her four-wheel-drive.

Both their vehicles were dust-covered, but hers looked like the dust might be holding it together.

"You drive that? I didn't know doctors believed in miracles. Tell me it runs better than it looks," he said. "Because it looks like you got it from Army surplus from World War II."

"It runs better than it looks." Her voice was uninflected.

"Thought doctors drove fancy cars."

"Wouldn't be real practical around here."

"Something about to fall apart's not practical, either. If you're stranded—"

"I won't be." She opened the bag with that distinctive sound.

"No fancy car and no black leather bag? You're not holding up the doctor image, you know."

"Backpack works better. Especially for wading through snow, climbing up or down, or otherwise doing things that need your hands free." She looked around, her gaze lingering on the barn, then the house. "And look who's talking about not holding up the image—rodeo star or tech entrepreneur."

"It'll come around. This is the start."

"I seem to remember you wanted the whole ranch. Not," she added quickly, "that there aren't better uses for your money."

She took out a kit that she put in one pocket, a flashlight in another pocket, quickly joined by a few pairs of medical gloves.

"You really think you'll need those?"

She closed the bag, then the door of the four-wheel-drive. "I probably need something stronger, but these might help. Tell me what you and Jarrod were you doing."

"My friend who drove the trailer here and I had offloaded the horses into that corral. My friend left. Jarrod and I started on the trailer. We'd mucked out the loose stuff. Then I was all the way in, pulling out hay from an overhead space up front. It was jammed in pretty tight. So I would pull it down and Jarrod would rake it over the edge into wheelbarrows."

"Okay, I'll take a look."

If that was supposed to dismiss him, freeze him out of joining her, screw that.

He detoured, grabbed two pairs of work gloves, then reached the back opening of the trailer and held out a hand to help her up.

She ignored his hand and stepped up into the trailer, looking around.

He joined her, holding out the work gloves. They'd be oversized on her, but they might help. She took them with a brief thanks, her gaze traveling around the inside.

"What was that you gave Jarrod that helped his breathing?" he asked.

"Beta-agonist bronchodilator," she said absently. "Tell me again what happened. From the start."

He recounted what they'd done, right up to when they met her coming toward them.

She listened without interrupting, nodding once when he finished.

"Did you have all the trailer windows open from the start?"

"Yeah." You'd have to be crazy not to. The more openings for the smell to get out the better.

She gave a sort of hum of confirmation and comprehension.

He remembered that sound. And how it had gotten him to talk that night.

That night...

She took one step forward, her gaze methodically covering the space. The step had taken her into a patch of light slanting through a window.

She seemed to shimmer. The way her skin had from the moisture still caught on it in that first moment he'd walked into the room that night.

That night…

Dust motes, just damned dust motes.

"Lot of dust in here," he said. "But that shouldn't be it or Jarrod would have trouble every single day on a ranch and he said he hadn't had any trouble for a long time. Shouldn't be what the horses left behind, either, because he's got to be used to that, right? And if it was hay he'd be sick all the time because there's no way he's not around hay. Any idea what it was?"

She slanted a look toward him. Possibly wondering why he'd started running at the mouth. "Not yet. This is your trailer?"

"No. Well, yes, now it is." Damned dust motes.

Another of those slanted looks.

"It was donated by a guy who inherited it and some horses from an uncle who'd been in rodeo. The nephew sent the horses and trailer together and said he never wanted to see any of them again. A buddy of mine volunteered to haul them here. We unloaded the horses, tended to them, then he was on his way, like I said."

She took out the flashlight and aimed it on some of that old hay he'd been pulling out. Some remained packed in the overhead space. She looked slowly and carefully.

She tucked the flashlight under her arm, snugging it against the side of her breast.

The way her breasts had felt under his hands, his mouth that night. *That night…*

"Want me to hold the flashlight for you?"

"No need."

Oh, hell, yes, there was need.

The work gloves joined the flashlight. She put on the medical gloves first, then pulled a work glove on over her right hand. Only then did she take the flashlight back into her left hand.

He thought he'd breathe easier then. His lungs thought otherwise.

She reached up and carefully detached five, maybe six pieces of hay and brought them down in front of the flashlight.

"Find something?"

And damned if she didn't make that humming sound again.

She moved the flashlight to get different angles on the hay. Then she tucked it under her arm again … against her breast. Her soft, curving breast…

She was getting out the kit, putting the hay in a small container apparently made from cardboard.

Concentrate on that, Halderman. Focus on that.

And then she said, "Ever hear of farmer's lung?"

"No."

"It's an allergic disease farmers get from inhaling mold spores that are on feed or hay that've had a lot of moisture in them. Hay with moisture, packed into an enclosed space, makes a perfect home for this mold. See that grayish powder on the surface?"

She moved the flashlight over the hay remaining in the overhead compartment. In the strong light he could see a sort of film in places that hadn't been visible with the minimal natural light.

"Yeah, but there's not much. And there wasn't all that much hay up there."

"Billions of those mold spores fit on the head of a pin. So figure how much was in the bit I'm going to have tested. Then look at what's still there." The flashlight went up, then down to what had spilled on the floor. "And what you'd already taken out. You breathe that in, it gets into your lungs and the mold spores have found nirvana. Not everybody gets sick, but those that do get sick show symptoms that a lot of people mistake for the flu. They think it will go away so they ignore it. That's the worst thing to do. Left untreated it becomes farmer's lung."

"You're saying Jarrod has farmer's lung?"

"More likely he had an allergic reaction to the mold spores. And I'm saying that you're very fortunate that he did."

"I was? Why?"

"Because he kept you from inhaling more. From your description you were practically inviting those mold spores into your lungs. Pulling them down into your face."

She reached up. For a flash he thought she was going to touch his face, and he wanted her to.

She reached higher, and brought a piece of hay down to his eye level. "At least your hat saved your from some of it."

What was he doing thinking he wanted her to touch his face … and with gloves on, no less.

"Good thing it's not bothering me at all, huh," he said, half thinking of her hand, her touch.

"We don't know yet."

How did she know—Oh, wait, she meant the mold spores. "Sure we do. I'm not having trouble breathing, no coughing."

"That was an acute allergic reaction because of Jarrod's asthma. You could still be affected. And it could go into farmer's lung. Let's get out of here."

Before he could gather enough wits to follow her she was already out of the trailer, had the gloves off and was tapping away at her phone.

"Onset of symptoms three to eight hours from exposure." She checked her watch. "It's been, what? At least an hour and a half? Probably more, since you two worked a while before Jarrod reacted. So, say one to six more hours to see if you develop symptoms."

"Symptoms like Jarrod had?"

"Probably not, unless you have asthma." She looked up. He shook his head. "Then more like the flu. Not everybody develops symptoms, so if you do it indicates a sensitivity. Huh."

"Huh, what?" He tried to get a look at her screen but the angle was wrong.

"Patients have gone into shock and died from their first exposure. At the very least, this initial case needs to be watched so you don't develop damage to your lungs."

CHAPTER TWELVE

"What does that mean?" he asked.

But she'd already hit a number from her contacts list.

"Connor?" She said into the phone. "It's Zoe Parisi. We've got a line on what might have caused this." She explained succinctly, then added, "Watch Jarrod for flu-like symptoms for the next six hours or so. Runny nose, fever, aching joints, things like that. Call me immediately if he shows any. … No, I think his allergic reaction got him out fast enough, along with having less exposure… Yes. Good. … Call any time."

Matt said, "So I watch for those symptoms, too, and when I don't have any after six hours, I'm okay to—"

But she was hitting another number. "Matty? It's Zoe… Yes. … Asthma attack, but he's good now, at home with his dad. … Yeah, I'm pretty sure I do. Mold spores in hay brought in with some horses to Pegasus Ranch. Connor's going to monitor Jarrod for the next six hours. But… Exactly. Right in the thick of it. Sucked in plenty. Need somebody to keep an eye on him for the next six hours to see if he develops symptoms. If he does, we'll have to have somebody with him overnight."

"Oh, c'mon," Matt protested.

She ignored him, still talking into the phone. "No, not contagious at all. … Uh-huh. … I guess so, but then I'll have to go. … Good. Yes. Bye."

"Why do I feel like I've had my life taken over?"

She grinned briefly, though she didn't look directly at him. "Because you have. Matty Currick will be here in about an hour and I'll stay until then. Matty can't stay the whole five hours, so—"

"I don't need—"

"—she's putting out the call to fill the rest of that time, plus for more later if it's needed. Which it will be if you develop symptoms."

"If it's like the flu—"

"With the potential to damage your lung capacity the rest of your life. We're not fooling with this." She looked up and met his eyes. It was a no-fooling look. "In the meantime, get out into fresher air."

"I better check those newcomer horses. Sounds like this could have hurt them."

"Ask your vet, but from what you said it was closed away from them during the trip, right? It was when you started pulling it out—after you'd offloaded them—that the spores were flying around."

"Come observe them, just in case."

"I'm not a vet and I need to make notes…" She gestured toward her four-wheel-drive. But her gaze went to the corral. She liked horses.

He had her.

"What if I show symptoms early and collapse out there?"

She rolled her eyes, but said, "Fine. I'll come look at your horses." She kept a good yard between them as they made the walk.

Purposely, he passed a closer entry to the near corral, continuing to the aisle between the corral fence and the fence of a small pasture that held two of the original arrivals. The rest were in a bigger pasture, but these two needed watching.

He left Zoe in the aisle as he entered the near corral, keeping his movements easy. Even so, the horses shifted away. He refilled the water buckets he'd set in place to track their consumption. Somebody wasn't keeping up, and he had a feeling he knew which one.

If it came to it, he'd separate them to be sure. But he'd rather not. They drew comfort from the familiarity of one another in these strange surroundings. Instead, he doctored the water and rejoined Zoe.

"I want to watch them a while," he told her.

"What did you put in the water?"

"Apple juice and electrolytes. Dehydration can be a problem from the travel. Plus, a lot of horses don't like strange water. Apple juice masks the flavor and most of them like it."

"It's the gray you're worried about?"

He looked at her, but she was watching the horses. "Yup. If he doesn't drink, I'll separate him and try hay soup."

"What a delicacy," she murmured, her gaze on the gray.

"His name's Knickerbocker."

"Will you adopt any out?"

"Not many if any. And you don't want that one. Most of ours are broncs. A few ropers, but mostly broncs."

"Ours?"

"Well, mine so far, but I hope to hire on help down the road."

She eyed the house and the barn again. He'd be willing to bet she wanted to say he could use help sooner rather than later, but didn't want to say anything he might interpret as encouragement to spend the money she had an eye on.

"Why broncs?" she asked neutrally.

"A lot of cowboys hold onto their own horses—steer wrestling horses or roping horses or barrel racing horses. After you spend years with a horse, you're going to retire it out where it can eat and roll to its heart's content. Some rough stock contractors are the same about their animals, but more rough stock slip through the cracks. So we're taking in more of them."

She considered. "At least you're not using that money to put in a Jacuzzi or something."

"Glad you approve," he said dryly.

"I wouldn't go that far. I like horses—I love horses—but the telemedicine project can save *people*'s lives."

"Can. Possibility," he said lightly. "I like the sure thing. I am saving horses' lives."

She tipped her head. "You like the sure thing? A rodeo cowboy?"

"Former."

The head tip deepened. "That's right. You quit."

"Retired. Got my company off the ground. And retired."

"Okay, I can see that's a tender spot. But—"

"Nothing tender about it."

"—you're really making their ends easier, not giving them a new lease on life. Like I said, a hospice for horses."

"Whatever you call it, Dr. Parisi, that's where the money is going. And that's the end of it. You're not getting your hands on it. Nobody's getting their hands on it."

She was going to say something more… And then she wasn't.

Good. Topic closed.

Zoe turned to look at the two horses in the next pasture. "That's a pretty one. The sorrel."

"Mean as a snake."

She laughed. And something went through him. She wasn't happy. Not happy at all that he wasn't handing over Harold Hopewell's bequest for her project. Yet she'd found amusement in what he'd said and let herself laugh. Nothing at all like the tears and drooping and recriminations of—

"You don't have to sound so happy about it," she said.

"Hey, he gave riders a chance for great rides … as long as they could hold on for eight seconds. Not many did with Python."

"Python? What kind of name is that for a horse?"

"It's a nickname. His real name's Montgomery something. So Monty. But he's mean as a snake, so Python—Monty Python."

"That sweet little thing's mean?"

"That's where people get fooled. Bareback broncs might be smaller, but they buck wilder. The bigger saddle broncs get into a rhythm that lets a cowboy sit up, keeping his feet going the way you have to. Lot of saddle broncs have draft horse in them, helps make them easier going. As for Python … watch this."

He clucked his tongue a couple times, a friendly invitation to come to the fence. Python pinned his ears back, snarled, and turned away.

Zoe chuckled. "Definitely not sweet and cuddly. But the other one—what's his name?—is coming over."

"That's Pizza."

"Pizza?" The horse broke into a trot at the sound of his name.

"Because that's what he made of several riders' faces." Matt dug in his pocket and found a baggy there still held one apple slice. The horse hung his head over the fence and snuffled. "See Pizza isn't such a bad fella, as long as you don't want to ride him. And most rough stock gets along with other horses. I've got two roping horses turned out in the main pasture with most of the retirees who came in that first day. Python's the exception. Pizza here's one of the few creatures he'll tolerate."

"Let me." She held out a hand and he gave her the apple slice.

"Flat of your hand," he instructed.

"I know."

She did it perfectly and Pizza took the treat gently.

"Now, with Python, you'd want your hand and arm in armor before you tried that. Maybe your head, too."

"Good to know. Your newcomer's drinking," she said in the same even tone.

Matt turned to look, slow and casual. Knickerbocker was, indeed, drinking with loud, slurping sounds from the apple juice-enhanced bucket.

"Up for a walk? From the top of that knoll—" He nodded toward it. "—you can see the whole layout."

They walked in silence. Atop the knoll, they could see the ranch road leading first to Pegasus Ranch, past the dry creek bed, then up to the H Bar H home ranch. He pointed out the other horses in a large pasture caught in the loop of that same dried creek bed. It twisted around and through much of the part of the ranch he owned now.

At the end of his pointing she looked at him, then away.

"What?"

"You didn't want all of the H Bar H back?"

He shrugged. "This corner was all Malloy would let go. But it has corrals and pastures. Plus the barn, and house."

She raised her eyebrows. "Yeah, those are a major selling point."

"They'll do for now. Turns out Pegasus Ranch is on land the first Halderman ranched here. Though that's not why I bought it. I'm not that sentimental. It works for the horses."

"Of course, a man who creates a hospice for rodeo horses wouldn't be sentimental."

He sidestepped that point. "Fair number of rodeo cowboys contribute one way or another to a peaceful retirement for the animals. But there's always room for more."

"And you wanted to do this."

"Yeah. I did."

She turned away. "Oh, look at the wildflower."

He frowned at the plant partway down the knoll, where flowers bloomed in a patch dug up by a fallen tree. "Is that blue weed? That stuff's bad for livestock and horses. If it's showing up here—"

"It's not blue weed. My grandmother knows this plant. Threadleaf something. A woman's name, I think. Like Clara. Something like that."

"It's just a weed."

"It's a wildflower and it's beautiful. Promise you won't yank it out or poison it. Every place should have flowers. Especially wildflowers."

"Fine." Before she could respond, he added, "Looks like Matty's truck."

They started down to meet her in the open area in front of the barn.

She got out of her truck and looked around, pitching her voice to reach them over the distance they still had to cover. "You know what this place needs? A dog. Maybe a couple."

Zoe grinned. "Matty's involved with dog rescue."

"I'll trade you a horse for two dogs," Matt said.

"Hah! We've already got our share of rescue horses. Have you met our foreman Jack Ralston? He swears they follow him home like lost puppies."

"A former rodeo bronc could round out your collection."

Matty turned to her. "You sure this man's sick? He seems to be well enough to dicker."

"Not sure he's sick at all. Just have to make sure that if he is, he gets the right treatment from the start."

"Okay, what do I look out for?"

Zoe listed dry cough, fever, chills, rapid breathing, rapid heart rate, joint achiness.

"You know," he offered, "I could look for those things myself and call if there's a problem."

They both looked at him an instant, then turned back to each other. "You know he wouldn't call, don't you?" Matty asked Zoe. "That pigheaded western I'm-stronger-than-any-germ attitude."

"Or in this case billions of mold spores. Which brings me to your other task. Make sure he doesn't even consider cleaning out that trailer."

"I could wear a mask. There's one around here somewhere and—"

Zoe kept talking to Matty. "Even if he isn't sensitive he'll need a good mask with fine enough filters to block mold spores. *Not* the kind kept around a barn somewhere. And if he *is* sensitive, it wouldn't be a good idea even with a mask."

"Oh, yeah, he'd think he could lick billions of mold spores easy."

"That's why you're here, Matty. I know I'm leaving him in good hands."

Zoe smiled and waved good-bye. He knew it was for Matty, but he enjoyed his share of it, too, as he watched her.

"Really, Halderman?" Matty asked.

For the first time in more years than he could remember he felt heat coming into this face. He'd been ogling Zoe's rear view as she walked to her vehicle.

"You know you're looking a little flushed," Matty added, having the maximum amount of fun at his expense. "Maybe we should check your temperature."

"Better use of my time is checking on these horses."

Because he already knew his temperature was rising. Just from watching Zoe.

Zoe sat at her desk in her tiny second-floor apartment, updating records, wishing she could be in bed.

Her bed. Alone. To sleep.

Ordinarily, she would have attended to the records sitting in her four-wheel-drive before moving on.

But today she'd been tempted by the possibility of seeing those horses.

When Matt talked about them, the coolness and distance in his brown eyes lifted.

Except for one moment.

Whatever you call it, Dr. Parisi, that's where the money is going. … You're not getting your hands on it. Nobody's getting their hands on it.

If he'd been cool when he spoke about her wanting the billionaire's money for the telemedicine program, it was that last sentence that had opened the door on the freezer.

What had that been about? It had been such a stark difference from his easy manner the rest of the time.

He clearly loved what he was doing.

Not that he was sentimental. Oh, no, of course not.

Having a piece of the Halderman ranch back—the original part— had to please him. Didn't it? The way he'd talked about growing up there and his dad that night.

That night…

That instant of waking and knowing he was gone. Completely gone. Cleared of his bag, his jacket, his clothes, *him*, the room had felt hollow.

So had she.

Eventually, she'd accepted that she'd made an error in judgment, and she'd learned from it. She'd faced the fact that he simply was self-centered. He'd gotten what he wanted that night and left.

In fairness, it wasn't his fault that he wasn't the person she'd thought he was—*fantasized* he was, really.

As she'd said in the diner, she'd too often seen what could happen to women who put fantasy ahead of good sense.

His showing up in Knighton this way had thrown her. But now she'd regained her balance. She wasn't a starry-eyed child any more. She was a doctor. With responsibilities.

She worked steadily for an hour before the question that had poked at her since that first day outside Taylor's office drummed too loudly to be ignored.

Do self-centered people start a horse hospice?

She didn't like the question. Because if he wasn't a self-centered jerk who had gotten what he'd wanted that night and left because that was his modus operandi, that meant he'd left *her.*

She shook her head, hard.

Face it. He had. He'd left her. After a night of love-making, he'd walked out. Wishing her the best like a birthday card from a distant relative.

You wouldn't really have wanted me to stick around that night.

It happened. It was over.

Back to work, Doc.

She wrote the technical terms, but what it boiled down to was a strong allergic reaction after a massive exposure to the irritant, resulting in the patient not being able to breathe. Immediate treatment was to get away from the irritant. Ongoing treatment meant avoidance of the source and a good dose of medicine.

Sort of the same way with her.

She'd once had an attack of not being able to breathe—or think—when exposed to a potent dose of Matt Halderman. Distance and medicine had set her right.

All she had to do now was stay away from the irritant.

Oh.

Could she have latched on to the idea of his donating as an excuse to...

Well, if she had, that was over. He'd made his position clear and—

Her phone rang.

"Zoe? It's Taylor. I'm at Pegasus Ranch. Matt's showing symptoms."

CHAPTER THIRTEEN

Taylor and her dog greeted Zoe at the door to the old house on Pegasus Ranch.

The house looked worse at night, perhaps because the scenery wasn't visible to distract from its worn and peeling exterior. The best feature was a porch that ran across the front, then turned and widened to cover the side of the house that faced the barn.

"He's dozing now," Taylor said quietly. "He was coughing. And he definitely has a fever."

"What's his temperature?" Zoe patted the collie's head. Sin always put himself into position for pats.

"He won't let me take it, but he's hot, he won't eat, and he's crabby, just like the kids when they have a fever."

Zoe nodded. Short of a thermometer, a mom was the best fever-testing tool around.

"I'd guess it's not real high," Taylor added. "But it's a definite change from when I relieved Matty. He was okay then. Worked quite a while on his computer—and, by the way, his Internet connection here has me drooling. The speed—Okay, I'll stop. But, really, you should try it. As time went on, he was more and more crotchety. This past hour, it's been steadily downhill."

Matt was stretched on a couch that appeared new and cheap. His cheeks were slightly flushed—so his blood was getting enough oxygen. He'd changed into a t-shirt and old jeans that were loose and faded nearly white. His hair was mussed, his mouth grim.

He looked so damned good.

Rainie was right. Matt's face wasn't symmetrical. And it wasn't just his nose. The left side was a bit shorter than the right side. Was it like palm reading, where the left side was supposed to be what you were born with while the right side was what you were making of yourself?

"Something between my teeth?" he growled.

She blinked. "No. How are you——?"

"Dirt on my face? Mustard from lunch? Grease from the truck?"

She'd been surveying him for medical reasons.

She'd been staring for other reasons.

"Why would you have grease? You haven't been out working on a truck, have you?"

"With your watchdogs tracking me? I meant the passenger compartment, not the engine. The truck that drove it here."

"No, he hasn't been working on a truck," Taylor said calmly. "I suspect he's referring to the dinner Rainie dropped off from the diner. He's been a little disjointed."

"I'm not disjointed. How's Jarrod?"

"No symptoms," Zoe said.

He grunted.

"That's good news." Taylor turned to the patient. "You told me you liked greasy food and then you didn't eat a bite."

"Couldn't stomach it."

Taylor lifted her brows slightly.

Zoe nodded. Loss of appetite.

She told Matt, "Get up and come over to the table where I can see you better."

Not only had the man not squandered money on a Jacuzzi, he hadn't spent any on the inside of this house, either.

It was clean. That was its high point. The kitchen might have been updated in the seventies, if then. A new microwave, a well-used coffee maker, and a TV sat on the counter.

There was the lightweight couch, a round dining table with a faded-to-mush flowered tablecloth, and two dining chairs. A corner desk that seemed to slant to the right held an impressive laptop and tiny printer.

The only light was an overhead fixture above the table and one of its bulbs was burned out.

He grunted as he sat up, then swung his legs around. Sin trotted over to him and stuck his nose in Matt's palm. Another grunt and he patted the dog.

A third grunt and he stood.

He was definitely aching.

Zoe stayed close enough to grab him if he started to topple, but she wanted to see how he negotiated the walk.

Not bad.

When he was seated, she took out the thermometer. The clinic had the quick-acting kind, but this was back to basics.

"Open your mouth."

"I don't need—"

She stuck it in his mouth and turned to Taylor.

"Since I might need to do horrible medical procedures to this patient, I think you and Sin should go."

"Very funny," Matt grumbled from the table.

Without turning to him she ordered, "Keep your mouth closed." Then resumed to Taylor. "I'll be here for a while and the next shift's at the top of the hour, so you might as well go."

Taylor smiled. "I appreciate the early release. I might be home in time to prevent chaos."

"Cal can't handle the kids?" That surprised Zoe.

"Most of the time. But the man cannot say no to ice cream—for himself or them—and then there are the sugar crazies at bedtime. It's not pretty." She slid a book and laptop into a bag and patted Matt on the shoulder as she passed him. "Bye, Matt. Hope you feel better. C'mon, Sin."

He mumbled something around the thermometer that an optimist could have taken as thanks.

"Thank you, Taylor," Zoe said aloud.

As the door closed, she took Matt's wrist to get his pulse. Faster than she would like.

She removed the thermometer. She'd expected worse considering the pulse.

"Not normal, but not bad. I need to listen to your heart and lungs."

He dragged his t-shirt up.

She knew human anatomy. His wasn't all that different from anybody else's. It wasn't.

Quickly she scanned for rash or other abnormalities. Concentrating. She put the stethoscope's earpieces in, placed the chest piece on his flesh, and listened.

A little fast, but steady.

"The back now."

He dropped the shirt in place and leaned forward. She pulled the back of his t-shirt up, again looking for anything unusual. Using the stethoscope, she heeded only the sounds and what they meant.

"Well, Doc?" he prodded when she'd dropped the shirt. He sounded strained.

"In layman's terms, not too bad."

"So, we can forget all this—"

"No. You have a fever. Once you show any symptoms, others can follow, so we're going to stay on top of this."

He muttered something under his breath. Still standing behind him, she had a straight view over his shoulder. He'd pulled the edge of the tablecloth over his lap.

Why…?

Oh. *Oh.*

The faded tablecloth wasn't long enough to cover an erection that the softened fabric of the jeans did nothing to hide.

Fever took on an entirely different meaning.

Zoe stepped back quickly, turning away to dig needlessly in her bag, letting that motion carry her along the edge of the table away from him.

"I believe it's a sub-acute, rather than an acute, reaction. But to be sure, as well as to guard against letting this slide into a chronic condition, you'll have someone with you overnight in case your symptoms worsen."

"You?" Did he sound worried that it would be her, or was she projecting her own feelings?

So what if he had a physical reaction to her.

That meant nothing, as she knew very well. He'd had plenty of physical reaction to her that night.

"No." She might have been a bit over-emphatic.

"Just give me a pill or something. I don't need anybody."

"I'd prefer not to give you anything that will suppress the fever. As long as it stays at this level it helps us monitor your system's reaction. But if it gets too high we will give you something. That's why someone's going to be here."

He grunted.

"You'll need to drink plenty of fluids and—"

"Not thirsty."

"Too bad." She opened the aged refrigerator, which protested such abuse. She felt on solid ground now that they were talking about treatment. "I guess it will be apple juice."

"I don't like apple juice."

"All you've got in here is apple juice."

"Uh-huh."

Ah. "All this is for the horses?"

"Yeah."

"Water it is, then."

She filled two of the largest glasses she could find and brought them back to the table, setting them in front of him.

She pulled the other chair to the far side of the table. "Drink."

CHAPTER FOURTEEN

"You're going to sit here and watch me drink water."

"Yes."

He took a swallow. "In silence." He wasn't making these questions because he felt no doubt.

"Unless you have something to say."

"I'm not a half-bad talker." He didn't feel like talking, so why was he volunteering?

"I'm sure. Probably learned it on the rodeo circuit."

"Yep."

She raised an eyebrow.

"You don't believe me? The boys—and girls—can keep their eyes and minds open just like anybody else. And they see a lot along the way. We didn't talk solely about who'd had the best ride, which animal was rank, and what brand of gloves get the best grip, you know."

"Okay, what did you talk about?"

"I'm not saying we *never* talked about those things. And some of the boys pretty much did limit themselves to those topics, along with—" He hesitated with his lips already forming a word. Thought better of it and opted for a generic substitute. "—other things. But there was a group I buddied with, who went beyond that. Guess that was Walker's influence."

"Walker? Walker *Riley*? The champion? You *knew* him?"

He frowned. "Never figured you to go all buckle-bunny about anybody."

"I'm not. I'd never—I never had one of those teen crushes on movie stars or singers. But Walker Riley." She might have sighed after saying the name. "And you knew him. Wow."

"Still do. Count him and Kalli as friends."

For a moment she looked at him without the glaze of suspicion and doubt that had been there from that first moment in Taylor's office.

For a moment she looked at him the way she had that night.

That night…

Before he'd walked out.

If he hadn't walked out, if he'd gone back…

There's time to go back, boy. Spend time with her, get to know her, see whether one thing leads to another. Plenty of time.

There'd been more Harold Hopewell had said. Something about a chance…

Because if you have a chance at the right kind of love, don't give that up for anything.

"You miss it," she said. "Rodeo."

That snapped him out of useless wondering.

"Miss the people, the excitement. Don't miss the pounding or always being in a different town."

She made that humming sound again.

He remembered how that sound felt when his lips were on her throat. How—

"Rodeo's different for some of the boys," he blurted to stop the memories. "They can't ever leave it. It's not just the competing, it's all of it. It's in their blood and bones. Walker's like that. Rarely competes anymore and only in roping events. But he runs the Park Rodeo. Has a small rough stock operation, too. But nothing that'll take him away from Kalli and the kids.

"Others love the competing, but they're okay with leaving when the time comes. They start getting a little long in the tooth for the circuit, but they've had fun, put some aside, and there's the family place they've been supporting to go back to. They're ready to leave rodeo and do something different. To raise a family if they haven't already started. They go and hardly look back.

"I wasn't like either group. Didn't want to spend all my life in rodeo.

Didn't want to ranch, either, not after—It wasn't for me. But there I was, with my teeth getting longer." He tried to grin. "The aches would only get longer, too. The rides shorter. The time to go was coming up, but what would I do? Didn't have a clue. Not until I started talking with Harold Hopewell."

"Drink."

As he did, he watched the haze seep back into her eyes.

She spoke evenly, "Walker Riley as your rodeo mentor and Harold Hopewell to fund your business venture. You've been very fortunate."

"You know you're not real subtle, Dr. Zoe Parisi. I caught the sting in the tail of those words. You're saying fortune's been kind to me and you're right. I've also worked damned hard. My rodeo winnings went into that venture. If it had failed, I'd be flat now. Walker and Kalli were good enough to show me the ropes early on and that was fortunate. But it's been a two-way street."

"Good for you, Matt. Really, I mean it. It's important to have good friends. Almost as important as being a good friend. But you've also had that billionaire starting—helping to start—your business and then, on top of that, inheriting money from him. And for what? Passing him the catsup? That truly is fortunate. Or lucky. Or whatever you want to call it. A lot of people don't have that in their lives. A lot of people have the opposite of that. They get cancer or liver disease or MS or something else that makes each day harder than you could imagine. And I see these people and I know I could do more for them if I just had the means. I'm not talking about unlimited amounts for untested treatments. I'm talking about a very specific program that doesn't cost the earth and beyond. It would tap into medical care that can turn lives around. Maybe save some, but for sure turn them around."

He wrapped his hand around the nearly empty glass. "And then along comes fortunate Matt Halderman with an inheritance that just landed in his lap. No work at all. That's what you're thinking."

"I shouldn't have—"

"It's committed, Zoe. If I'd known about your program when I first got the letter about Harold's will... Maybe not then, either. Because the letter said things—things about what we'd talked about that night and I owe it to Harold to honor his wishes."

She looked at him, studying him. Her suspicion and doubt weren't gone, but they had faded a bit.

Problem was, there was nothing like the glow—the glow for him— he'd seen there that one night.

Nothing at all like it.

She nodded. "Okay, Matt. I won't bother you about it again."

She started to turn.

Automatically, he reached toward her. His hand brushed her arm. She went sideways to sever the connection. His hand dropped.

"It's not bothering me. Seeing you is not bothering me, Zoe."

She looked over her shoulder at him. "Then you're fortunate again. I hear the next shift arriving. I'll go bring them up to date on my way out. Good night, Matt."

CHAPTER FIFTEEN

Matt felt something like horror when he saw who walked in as his next watchdog.

Ruth Moski.

Zoe's grandmother, for Pete's sake.

"I really don't need any help." He started to rise. "I'll just go tell Zoe and you can leave—"

"Sit."

He sat.

"She's gone." She took the glass from him on her way to the sink.

"She couldn't have. I didn't hear that coffee grinder she drives."

Ruth got a fresh glass, filled it and brought it back. "She's gone and she didn't fly. Now, drink."

"That thing she drives should be sent to a good home to die peacefully like the horses here."

Ruth Moski gave him a slit-eyed look. "It runs."

"Barely."

"You're confusing the inside with the outside. Lisa Currick's husband Shane Garrison spent a good part of their spring trip here giving it a good going over. He knows what he's doing."

"Come's a point when even the best mechanic can't keep something going. Why doesn't she save up and—"

"Save up? She did. You know why Zoe's still driving that thing? Because she put everything she'd saved up for a new vehicle into that fund for the remote doctoring. Had this big, long explanation about how it would save wear and tear on her vehicle so she didn't really need a new one. Real reason is she wants what's best for her patients. Even the ones who don't deserve it."

He opened his mouth, then closed it. When you were eating arena dirt there was no sense pretending the bronc hadn't thrown you.

Ruth added, "Time for you to be in bed. Where are your pajamas?"

"Pajamas?" he repeated.

She headed toward the back of the house.

He got up and followed as self-protection. But while she marched briskly ahead, it was as if he were wading through mud.

She flipped on one light, turned it off. Did the same in the next empty bedroom and finally came to the one he was using. She made a disapproving sound.

So his bed wasn't made. What was the point when you just got back into it at night?

"Where are your pajamas?" She started opening drawers in the dresser.

"Mrs. Moski."

"Oh, for heaven's sakes. Sit down before you fall down." She pushed him to the edge of the bed, which was the only place to sit in the room. "I can't find any pajamas."

"I, uh, I don't wear them."

"What's that to get all red in the face about? What do you—? Oh. Well, for heaven sakes, you're not the first one I've encountered in my life, you know. But you're not sleeping naked tonight. Not while I'm here caring for you. You got a pair of sweatpants?"

"Suitcase. In the closet."

She retrieved them. Shook them out with a disapproving sound, then handed him a clean t-shirt, and ordered, "Into the bathroom. Change. Wash up, too. You'll feel better. If you don't wash up I'll do it for you. Don't think I won't."

He believed her.

But washing up was more of a chore than he'd experienced without having broken bones involved.

He came out at last, thinking bed was a really good idea.

She'd remade the bed. She'd done other things, too, though he wasn't quite sure what. Except the room looked like it had been hit by a tornado. Some sort of reverse tornado that picked up and put away.

"You shouldn't have—"

"Well, I did. Get in bed instead of standing there weaving."

As soon as he sat on the edge of the bed, she stuck a thermometer in his mouth. Zoe must have inherited the technique from her.

"Swing your legs up."

These had to be the same sheets on the bed because he only had one set. But somehow they felt fresh and new when he slid in.

She pulled the blanket up to his chest, then added a quilt she must have brought herself, because it wasn't his.

She took out the thermometer with one hand and handed him a water glass with the other. "Drink."

Like granddaughter, like grandmother.

Except Ruth Moski started to tip the glass so he either drank or drowned. He drank.

She muttered at the thermometer but didn't share with him. He wasn't asking.

"You might get chills during the night. Any time you wake up, take a drink."

She'd brought one of the chairs in to serve as a bedside table and had a glass and two jars of liquid on it—water and apple juice—along with a flashlight.

"I'll be in the living room. If you need help getting to the bathroom, call—"

"I won't need—"

—out. Or if you're feeling worse. And don't go all modest on me, understand? I'll be back in to take your temperature regular. Don't make a fuss and it'll go easier. Anything else you need now?"

"Nothing. Thank yo—"

"Don't thank me. I know you did something to my Zoe."

That left him with his mouth open and no words coming out.

"Hurt her somehow. Sit up," she ordered. He did. "Not that she'd ever admit such a thing to me or you or anyone else. Sit back. But I can see it. Knew it when she came back from that trip those years ago. Always wondered… Then here you come sashaying into town and I knew. Same look. Right there in those honest eyes of hers. That means I might not fluff your pillows—"

Though she just had.

"—but don't worry I'll be feeding you poison, either. I won't. So no need to chat or charm, but you don't have to worry about what you eat or drink with me. I might be tempted just a little, but I couldn't face your daddy in the hereafter if I did such a thing. Even though I suspect he'd agree with me. He was a fine man."

Now Matt's head really hurt.

"Mrs. Moski—"

"You're old enough to break my Zoe's heart, you're old enough to call me Ruth."

"I never meant—"

"You should be sleeping." She walked out, but didn't close the door.

He'd been aware of Ruth Moski a few times during the night. Twice to take his temperature and at least once holding on to him as he stumbled to the bathroom. Thank God she hadn't come in. Not that he remembered, anyway.

She was gone when he woke up to full sunlight.

In her place, Doc Johnson stood beside his bed, presenting a thermometer and telling him to open up.

As he did, he caught sight of Zoe standing at the end of the bed. She didn't meet his gaze.

Doc chatted away about Ruth being a good nurse and Matt being an idiot until it was time to remove the thermometer. He glanced at it then handed it to Zoe.

"I don't know why you wanted me to come out here, Zoe. You've got everything in hand."

But Matt knew why. It was so she didn't have to be alone with him. So she didn't have to touch him again. Even with a stethoscope, as Doc was doing now.

So she didn't risk him reacting that way to her touch again.

That pretty much proved Ruth's theory was hooey. Zoe wanted nothing to do with him.

Maybe she'd been hurt when he left that night, but she sure as hell wasn't pining for him now. That was clear as ice.

"You have so much more experience with this, Doc," she was saying. "I wanted to be sure…"

"Well, be sure. You've done everything you should do for this patient, and he's heading the right direction. Most cases only think to come to the doctor long after." He looked down at Matt. "You're a very lucky young man—"

Her head came up and their eyes met for an instant before she looked away again.

Seeing you is not bothering me, Zoe.

Then you're fortunate again.

Because seeing him *was* bothering her. He'd gotten that even in his fevered state last night.

Because he'd hurt her in the past.

But did that—could that—mean she felt anything for him now?

"—that Zoe—Doc Parisi—is so smart and recognized the potential for this immediately."

"Yes, sir."

"You heard about this telemedicine program she's working so hard to get us? It'll be a great thing—great thing—when we can get it up and running."

Matt flicked a look toward her, but she wasn't returning this one. "Yes, sir."

Doc Johnson patted Matt's shoulder. "Rest a couple more days. Stay in bed 'til tomorrow morning. Then the rest of tomorrow go real easy."

"But I'm okay on my own now?"

"Fever's down, so I'd say so. Dr. Parisi?" She gave a single nod. "You'll only need watching if you're a darned fool and I don't think you will be."

"My horses—"

"Taken care of," Zoe said flatly.

Before he could question that, Doc Johnson was going on. "After these next couple days, then your primary issue will be avoiding re-exposure. You do that and you should be just fine. You've always been good and healthy—accidents every time I turned around from some daredevil trick or another, destined for the rodeo from the time you were in diapers—but not much sickness. Why, I remember when you were five and your mother had you in Van Hopft Pharmacy. Took one look and knew you had scarlet fever. Clear as day. The rash, the flushed face, the strawberry tongue—you had it all. But she didn't have an inkling, because you were always so healthy."

Doc chuckled. "She was heading for Jefferson to get a dress for some party and she couldn't believe you were really sick, not her healthy boy. I took you off to the office, got you started on the antibiotics, and by the time she picked you up on her way back from Jefferson, you were already starting to feel better."

A sound or a movement from Zoe drew Matt's attention, but she showed nothing now.

"Ah, Veronica Halderman," Doc Johnson said mistily. "Your mother is the most glamorous creature Knighton has ever seen. How is she these days?"

"I believe she's fine, sir."

"Still living in Montana?"

"No, they moved to Palm Springs some time ago."

"Ah, well, Palm Springs. That should match her glamour."

"Yes, sir."

"Well, please give her my kind regards next time you talk to her, should she recall rusty old Doc Johnson."

"I will, sir. I'm sure she'll remember you."

Both doctors started out.

Matt said, "Zoe," even though he knew she didn't want to stay.

Yet she did.

Doc Johnson waved from the door. "I'm going to the clinic now.

See you later, Zoe. And next time I see you, Matt, I expect you to be in fine fettle."

Reluctantly, Zoe came back halfway to his bedside.

"Who's taking care of the horses?"

"Malloys are doing most of it. Jack Ralston's helping out. Other people filling in."

"You?"

"A lot of people. Listen, eat some of this fruit—" She pointed to a bowl that had joined the water on his bedside chair. The apple juice had disappeared. Another plate was wrapped in plastic. "—and there are sandwiches. Rainie will come by with some dinner. Salad and chicken. Nothing greasy."

"Thanks."

"Lots of people are—"

"I know. Lots of people are helping and I'll thank them all, including your grandmother who scares the living daylights out of me. Right now I'm thanking you, so suck it up and take it, Parisi."

She'd started to smile a little at his confession about Ruth. "You're welcome. Your biggest thank you will be following instructions."

His brain must still be fevered, because all he could think about at the moment was that the instructions included staying in bed all day, which he wouldn't mind at all if she joined him.

Definitely fevered. Good thing they weren't taking his temperature or pulse right now.

He became aware that Zoe was lingering—clear proof his thoughts weren't transparent or she'd be gone like a shot.

Soon, he was aware of a fierceness rising up in her. A fierceness he didn't understand. Especially since, when she spoke, her voice was one shade softer than neutral.

"I remember your dad. He had the greatest smile. And when he laughed, everybody laughed with him."

She started to walk out.

"What else?" He had to swallow. "What else do you remember about him?"

"I remember that time he'd won a prize at the fair—was it county or—"

"State."

"Oh, yes, the state fair. You'd just rolled back into town from Douglas and he started loading people—kids—into the back of your truck and when it was full he told the rest to come on to the pharmacy and he treated every single one of us to an ice cream cone."

She smiled, looking fully at him for the first time today. And he smiled back. The warmth of his father's hand on his shoulder that day felt again like a real presence.

And his voice. "We did it, son. We did it."

CHAPTER SIXTEEN

Matt woke from a nap. A fever that had nothing to do with illness held him.

He'd been dreaming. Dreaming a memory.

That night…

Propped up by pillows, her tucked into the curve of his arm, her head tipped back against his shoulder, leaving his mouth more room to taste her throat, her shoulder.

"You've changed a lot," he'd said.

She'd chuckled. "Well, thank you, because I was an awkward, dreamy kid with no coordination and thick glasses."

"As I said, you've changed a lot." His voice deepened. "And I'm here to say you've got just the right coordination."

She smiled and said, "I remember you."

That threw him.

Most women would have angled for more compliments on how good they looked now. They sure wouldn't admit to remembering him when he wasn't as clear about remembering them. Or should it be *girl* in Zoe's case… No, not girl. Because there was a wisdom there… Oh, hell, his thoughts snarled so bad he couldn't get a word out.

"But then you disappeared from one summer to the next," she said.

"Dad was killed the September I was fifteen. Hit by a drunk driver when he was helping a woman with a flat tire."

"Oh, Matt. Oh, no. How could I not have known?"

"You were a kid."

She looked up at him and he forgot that he hated sympathy, that he never talked about this.

"Then the ranch went. She sold it. He was hardly in the ground and she sold the ranch that had been in our family for generations. It all happened fast. By Christmas she needed 'a break,' and went on a cruise."

"*She* went? What about you?"

"I stayed at the ranch. We had horses and stock to sell. She came home—back—with a new husband."

She sucked in a breath.

"Moved to Montana then. The two of them thought they'd get to be pals with the Hollywood folks living there. I got out as soon as I could, took to the rodeo circuit."

"You don't see them?"

"Not much."

"Matt…"

He'd changed the subject then. By touch, rather than words.

Stroking over that so-soft skin of her breasts, teasing the tips to points that turned the teasing around on him, shifting their bodies into alignment, requesting entrance to her. Receiving the heated, silken welcome that left no thoughts, only her.

Zoe stabbed a pen into a notepad.

She'd thought that by accepting that he was not going to donate to the telemedicine program that she could shift to a cool, impersonal approach with Matt Halderman.

Took one look and knew you had scarlet fever. Clear as day. The rash, the flushed face, the strawberry tongue—you had it all. But she didn't have an inkling…

Doc Johnson was a dear man and a good physician. How could he have been so dazzled by Veronica Halderman's "glamour" not to have seen?

Scarlet fever with its distinctive rash and high fever … and its potential for long-term damage. How could a mother who was paying attention not notice?

A mother who left her child with scarlet fever at the doctor's office so she could get a party dress.

A mother who sold her son's birthright.

She sold it. He was hardly in the ground…

A day in bed, yes. But not at all the way he'd fantasized about.

After most of the day napping—though he'd had a visit from Jarrod Malloy and Midnight—followed by a good night's sleep, Matt figured he was back to himself.

There was something that kept tapping at the back of his mind. Something to do with Zoe. Trouble was, whenever he tried to pull it to the front of his mind other aspects took over. Like those dreaming memories. Like the way she'd looked with dust motes turning her golden. Like the lightest touch of her fingers to his skin.

And that left this whatever-it-was stuck in the back of his mind.

Especially after a shower wiped him out.

He rested a bit before getting dressed and fell asleep a while after.

He was vaguely aware of faint noises beyond the closed bedroom door for quite a while before they made him curious enough to get up and investigate.

He negotiated the hallway pretty damned well if he said so himself.

Until he reached the living room.

He stopped dead.

Taylor Larsen Ruskoff was stepping down from a mini-ladder, while Val Trimarco fluffed out curtains at one side of the window overlooking the front porch.

Curtains that had not been there last time he'd looked.

Bright pillows tumbled on the sofa and one of those handmade small blanket things rested on an arm. Tables with lamps flanked it. An easy chair he'd never seen before sat beside a short bookcase with a tall lamp behind them. The chair and sofa faced the TV, now sitting on a chest.

There were four new chairs around the table and a new tablecloth covered it, with a plant in a pot in the middle.

"What the he—Uh, what happened?"

"Oh, good, you're up, so we can get into the bathroom and bedroom," Taylor said.

By now his gaze had taken in the kitchen. The microwave had been mounted on a wall. Without that and the TV it almost looked spacious, even with another bowl of fruit on the counter.

"What happened here?" he repeated.

"We're making it livable," Val said cheerfully.

"It was clean." He turned to Taylor. "The people you hired did everything I asked."

"I know," she said, disapproving. "Basic."

"I'm okay with basic."

Val clicked her tongue. "There's basic and then there's sub-basic. Or in this case, sub-, sub-, sub-basic."

"Here, sit down," Taylor said.

He was too stunned to resist when she guided him to the couch. From here he could see another new lamp—a stubby one on top of the refrigerator. Leaning against one of the new chairs was a stack of framed items.

He pointed. "What's that?"

"Art for the walls. Didn't want to hang them without your input," Val said.

"But deciding that is all you have to do today," Taylor said.

"Right. Just sit back and relax. You won't even have to worry about being exposed to that mold again. Not anytime soon."

"What do you mean?"

"I mean they're cleaning that trailer."

"Zoe—?"

"No. Not once she made sure they had the right equipment. After that, she and Jack saddled up a couple of your horses—"

"*What?*"

He stood up fast. Taylor put a hand on his shoulder to push him back down. Truth to tell, it didn't take much, because his knees missed the memo about holding him up.

"They're mixed in with broncs—"

"Don't be insulting, Matt," Val said. "If you don't think my Jack can tell the difference between a saddle horse and a rodeo horse, you and I are going to have a long discussion, which I guarantee I'll win. Zoe knows, too," she added, as if Zoe were an afterthought, which didn't sit well. "She's a very good rider. Unlike me, though I *am* getting better. Give me another decade and I'll be decent," she finished cheerfully.

"You're looking worn out, Matt," Taylor said.

"Probably all my talking. Sorry," Val said. "We're going now. Sit here and rest while we tackle the bedroom and bathroom. Though you could look through the artwork if you want, pick the ones you like, so we can hang them. Or maybe later. We're going to go. Right now."

It wasn't quite that fast.

By the time they closed the bedroom door, leaving the living room quiet, he decided just to put his head back on the sofa cushion and rest his eyes.

CHAPTER SEVENTEEN

"C'mon, Matt. It's lunch time."

He still felt half asleep. "Where?" The only food in sight was the bowl of fruit on the counter. But he could swear he smelled food. Real food. It smelled good.

"It's a rare warm, sunny day this spring, so we're out on the porch," Val said.

"I'm not that hungry."

Then he thought he heard a voice outside…

"You're coming and you're eating," Taylor said firmly. "From the evidence around here you've been living on water and sandwiches."

"Salad wasn't even touched," Val said.

"All right, all right," he grumbled, but with a bit of a smile as he let them herd him out the back door.

He blinked at the daylight and at the people.

"Come sit here," Taylor said, guiding him from behind as if he were an invalid.

"I'm okay. I—"

"Sit," Ruth Moski said.

He sat.

The table in front of him was loaded with food. Fried chicken. That's what he'd smelled. "Where'd this all come from?"

"Here and there," Matty said.

He looked beyond the porch. "What's going on?"

The donated trailer was out of the barn, sitting in full sun with every door and window wide open. It appeared to have just been washed.

"Zoe had us clean out the trailer under strict guidelines," Dave said.

"Masks, lots of ventilation, wet it down first, bagged up everything to be burned away from people or animals—good thing there wasn't a lot of it—and special cleaners. When we were done with that fun, we had to pack up the clothes we wore for the work, shower out in the barn and put on clean clothes."

"Simple precautions," Zoe said from the opposite end of a long table that had been set up.

"Yeah, notice she managed to get herself assigned to checking on the horses," Matty said.

"Jack needed help," Zoe said with only a small grin. "And you and Dave and Cal did a great job on the trailer. It's squeaky clean now."

"You did all that? I could have—"

"No," they chorused in response. Dave added, "Ruth and Hugh had the toughest job, keeping the kids out of trouble.

Ruth snorted. Hugh said nothing, because he was asleep on a lounge chair in the sun with two kids napping on his lap and a third curled up by his legs.

The older kids, accompanied by the dog Taylor had brought the other night and a second dog of broad-minded parentage, leaped around Cal as he emerged from the barn in clean clothes.

"We fed the kids and Hugh first," Matty said. "Works great with Hugh and the little ones, but it just refuels the older kids."

Jack joined the group and Matt saw him talking to the kids, who nodded their understanding.

Cal shooed them all toward the dried creek bed down by the ranch road, with the dogs on their flanks.

As Jack and Cal came up to the porch, Matt thanked them, too. They shrugged it off.

"The kids know these horses aren't like they're used to?" he asked.

"They know," Cal said.

"Plus, Cal redirected them," Jack added.

"Told them to look for Indian arrowheads in that creek bed."

"Never heard of arrowheads being found there," Matt objected.

"They don't know that," Cal said.

"Good move," Dave said. "They'll have a great time searching."

"Time to eat," Ruth announced.

Matt was relieved to see everyone else obeyed her orders nearly as quickly as he did.

After the flurry of plate-fillings and people finding spots to sit, each group of workers filled the others in on what they'd done.

"You're going to need a new tire on the trailer's right rear," Cal said.

Matt nodded. "I'll see to that next week."

"That's a nice gray that Zoe rode," Jack said. "Nice motion."

"Roo. Short for Kangaroo."

From talking about Roo and his other roping horse Russ, he and Jack discussed whether Python could be trusted with the main herd, and agreed no. That meant Pizza was denied more companionship for now, and Jack suggested giving him a few hours a day with the big group.

Then Val and Taylor described what they'd done. "But we still need Matt to select artwork so that can be hung," Val finished.

"Yeah, I wanted to ask about all that stuff inside. Where'd it all come from? You folks—"

"Here and there," Matty repeated with a grin, talking over his protest that they shouldn't have brought or done so much. "Just be grateful my in-laws are visiting their daughter and her family in New York or you'd have been scooped up and carried off."

"When are Donna and Ed coming back?" Val asked.

"Next month."

That led to discussion of when the spring roundup and branding might happen, with true spring taking its time arriving this year. It had been so chilly the snowmelt was later and slower than anyone could remember.

A dark blue pickup pulled in at a sedate pace. Everyone waved, while Matty and Taylor went to greet the new arrivals.

"Who... Reverend Foley's still here?" Matt asked as he recognized the man walking around the front of the truck to the passenger door.

"It wouldn't be Knighton without Ervin Foley," Dave said.

His passenger's head barely showed over the dashboard. A child, perhaps. But a white-haired child?

The minister took something from his passenger and handed it to Taylor. A blue covered cake plate.

Matt knew that plate. He was sure he knew it…

"The *Widow Brontman?*"

"Still going strong," Dave confirmed.

"She's got to be a hundred." Matt heard a note of awe in his own voice.

"Ninety-three. Bereavements and illnesses keep her going," Ruth said.

"Grandma," Zoe admonished.

"It's a fact. If she didn't have funerals and sicknesses as a reason for making her rum cake, she'd just stop breathing." Ruth considered that a moment. "The rum she drinks while making it might help, too. Sort of a preservative."

That drew laughter.

"I remember that rum cake," Matt said. "Very fondly. Eating it's probably the first time I—uh…"

"Became inebriated," supplied Dave. "Join the club."

"Nearly knocked me on my—" Cal shot a look toward Ruth and substituted. "—uh, flat the first time I had it. Tastes so good it sneaks up on you."

There were murmurs of agreement as they stood to welcome the arrivals.

"Matt, my boy," Reverend Foley said, taking his offered hand in both of his. "Welcome home."

He was saved from trying to think of what to say after "good to see you" by an insistent tug on his arm.

"You should be resting, young Halderman. You look weak as a kitten. Sit right down."

The only way to soothe Mrs. Brontman was to obey. Someone drew up a chair for her nearby.

She handed him a piece of rum cake. That suited him fine. He ate the first mouthful with pleasure and was digging the fork into the second moist bite when Matty distracted Mrs. Brontman on one side of him and Taylor swooped in on the other side and took the plate out of his hand.

"Fever," she murmured as she kept going.

He turned his head in pursuit of the cake and saw her hand it off to her husband, who put down his own already empty plate and smiled at her with a "Thanks."

Cal should have been thanking *him*, since it was his cake.

Taylor said, "I need a volunteer to bring out the artwork so Matt can make his choices before he falls asleep again."

"I'm not going to fall—"

"I'll do it." Jack followed Taylor inside.

"If you're not going to take an afternoon nap," Dave said, "I'll do it for you. After all that lunch and Mrs. B's delicious cake, I'm ready for a siesta."

"Oh, but Matt doesn't have any cake," the widow said. "How could I have forgotten to give you a piece?"

"You did give me one, but—"

"Here," she said, handing him another plate with a huge piece of cake. "That should hold you a while."

He dug in quickly. This time he got two forkfuls before Val plucked it away while the reverend was talking to the widow.

"Hey," he protested.

Val paid no attention, but went to hold the door open with her free hand as Jack and Taylor came out with the framed artworks. As soon as Jack put down his load, Val handed him the cake plate.

Fever or no fever, Matt was catching on to something going on. With looks and small gestures a conspiracy operated right out in the open. He wasn't sure what all of it was about, but he saw Matty cutting additional slices of the cake and wrapping them in plastic. Ruth tucked the plastic covered slices into various storage containers. They were going to have the plate cleared in short order.

"There," Taylor said, having leaned the frames against the edge of the table so he could see them. "Now you can pick."

Zoe *ooohed* her admiration from off to his right.

"Val took all those," Jack said with pride.

As everyone gathered closer, Mrs. Brontman clicked her tongue at Matt.

"You've got your fork, but you don't have any cake. Not even a plate."

Her tone made him feel like he'd been so careless he might not be trusted with a plate.

"Sorry," he mumbled, watching looks zing around among the women.

"My goodness, this is the last piece. You all have gone right through this cake. I should have made two," Mrs. Brontman said with pride. "It's fitting the last piece goes to you, Matt."

He agreed. "Thank you," he said warmly and dug in.

This time, he saw it coming. Ruth put an arm around the widow, redirecting her focus.

Zoe moved in close to the artwork, which also brought her near him. "Oh, Val, these are amazing."

She reached for his plate. He pivoted away, eating fast.

"All taken in Lewis and Clark counties." Val sounded as if she were fighting the giggles.

Zoe got a hold of his plate and tugged. He held on, forking more cake into his mouth.

Ruth called the reverend over to where she and Mrs. Brontman stood, then looked over her shoulder at them and frowned fiercely.

"The colors are fabulous," Zoe said out loud. She dropped her voice. "Give me that plate, Matt. You shouldn't have alcohol with a fever."

"There is something about the light in Wyoming." Val was definitely fighting the giggles. "It's like soft crystal."

Dave was chuckling and Jack, Cal, and Matty were grinning.

Zoe was not.

"It will dehydrate you and I will pour water down your throat until you drown," she threatened in whisper.

"That should cure him," Taylor murmured.

Matt was losing the tug-of-war over the plate—he preferred to think it was because she had a better angle than because he truly was as weak as a kitten.

Just before Zoe wrested it from him, he stabbed a good quarter of the piece with his fork and held on to it, holding it aloft like spoils. Zoe made a grab for it, but he turned in the chair just enough to block her as he put the whole thing in his mouth.

"You capture the different moods of the landscape so well, Val," Taylor said, more loudly than usual, covering some of the noise they made.

Val sucked in a breath, apparently trying to even her voice. "I'll never get all the different moods. But thank you. I wanted to show some of the diversity."

"Come see the photos Val took, Reverend Foley, Mrs. Brontman," Taylor invited, now that the battle of the plate had ended.

Ruth gave them all a daunting stare as she, too, joined the group looking at the framed photos, but the only one who seemed to take it to heart was Zoe.

She picked up the discussion with determination, pointing out landmarks in the various photos.

She also took the fork out of his hand and replaced it with a glass of water.

Val Trimarco was a gifted photographer. The photos caught the contradictory impressions that these combinations of rock and sky and water had endured for centuries and yet changed instant to instant.

"May I have that one?" Matt asked, pointing to a shot that gave a man's eye-view up a rock wall to impossibly blue sky.

"You may have them all," Val said. "Or none. In other words, take as many as you want."

He selected three others—one with shadows of horses moving across the ground, a wide vista, and clouds rolling in like waves.

"Now," Matty said, "you need something to continue the work Taylor and Val have done in brightening up this place. What do you think of these?"

She moved the landscapes he hadn't selected to one side, revealing a series of close-ups of flowers. "How about these for the hallway?"

Zoe's breath of admiration was even longer this time.

"These are stunning. That's fireweed, right?" She pointed to a tall plant with rosy petals along its spikes.

"First one to come back after a burn," Cal said, exchanging a look with his wife that made her cheeks go pink.

"We'll, uh… Cal and I'll go hang the ones you picked," Taylor said.

They disappeared inside with the landscapes. Matt wasn't convinced they'd spend all their time hanging pictures.

Zoe pointed to another. "The red one's Indian paintbrush, of course. Gorgeous."

"State flower of Wyoming," Dave said.

"You remember that from school?" Matt asked.

"Hey, that's not *that* long ago. Besides I've had more recent reminders." Standing behind Matty, he put his arms around her, crossing them at her waist.

She smiled up at him. "It was my wedding bouquet."

"Yellow monkeyflower," Val said, pointing to a sunny patch dominating another photo. "We planted them everywhere last year. And they did not take over everything, despite Jack's worries about them being invasive."

He smiled at her. "They've grown on me."

"We're going to plant more, this year. Lots more. I love them," Val said. "And this other yellow one that looks like a daisy is bur marigold."

Matty patted her husband's arm. "That's the design Lisa uses for her jewelry business. She and Shane have a metal sculpture of it over the fireplace in their place in New York."

"These are spectacular. Not that I don't like the landscapes, Val, but these…" Zoe stepped back, taking them all in.

Val grinned. "I'm partial to them, too. Though these might be too big for a hallway. Let me experiment with smaller versions and I'll bring them by later, Matt. You can look at them without any pressure."

"He's not partial to wildflowers," Zoe said.

"That's not—"

"We saw a wildflower the other day. Over by that knoll. A wildflower," she repeated with emphasis, not looking at him. "*Not* a weed. I couldn't remember the name. Grandmother, you know the one. Blue, sometimes more lavender, usually with white in the center."

"This time of year, most likely threadleaf phacelia," Ruth said.

"That's it. I knew you'd know. I kept thinking it was something-Clara, but it's Celia."

"I'm not familiar with that one. Would you mind if I come take photos of it, Matt?" Val asked.

"Any time."

Zoe gave him a sharp look. "Time for you to rest."

"I'm fine. I'm…"

But no one was listening to him.

Faster than he could have believed, they had food put away in his fridge, table and chairs stowed in the various vehicles, and tools put back where they came from.

The Reverend Foley and Mrs. Brontman left first. Then Ruth and Hugh, followed by Taylor, Cal, their kids, and dog.

Matt was ordered inside. He was aware of more look-orders being given. Jack and Dave stayed close by as he made his way to a chair at the table. Zoe gave them a confirming nod and placed another glass of water in front of him.

He tried to say thank yous and was firmly hushed by everyone. Heck, he thought one of kids told him to stop, to sit down, to drink his water. Could that have really been little Addie Trimarco?

With final good-byes, the Curricks, Jack and Val and Addie were gone.

Only Zoe remained. She sat across from him. "Finish that water. You had too much rum cake for a man with a fever."

"Fever's almost gone. That cake was really good." And, yes, left a bit of a buzz.

"Very dehydrating."

She was studying him professionally. He smiled at her. That made her look away.

"Why'd you do all this, Zoe?"

"I didn't do all—"

"You got it rolling. The horses, the trailer, in here."

"Everybody pitched in. *I'm* not trying to be the lone ranger saving all the old rodeo horses around without any help."

"No, you're trying to save all the people of Lewis and Clark counties. So how can you criticize me?"

She tipped her head and made that humming sound. The buzz in his head settled lower.

"I don't think I'm criticizing you, exactly." She stood. "You need rest. And drink more water."

He'd been wrong. Really wrong about her.

That instant in Taylor's office when he'd acted like she wanted the money for herself. Just because … other people did, he shouldn't have assumed she did.

That something at the back of his mind tapped again. But he had no brain cells to wrestle with it.

Sleep was rolling in fast.

Could he have been wrong about Zoe the first time, too?

That night…

That night when he'd turned back to see her sleeping and was so sure he was doing the best thing when he pulled the door closed behind him.

CHAPTER EIGHTEEN

Doc Johnson had been out to see him again, this time without Zoe.

Matt had reported in once to the clinic, where he saw Doc Johnson, his long-time nurse Della, equally long-time clinic manager Polly, and not a glimpse of Zoe.

The Malloys, father and son, helped daily with the horses for a full week. Jarrod still pitched in nearly every day.

Cal and Taylor came by with a set of porch chairs they asked if he wanted. Jack dropped off harness he said he didn't need any more. Dave brought a tack board he said the Slash-C was replacing.

Val brought him lunch one day, along with a lineup of those flower pictures on a rough board. He hadn't expected to like flowers in his hall, but he did like this. He liked it a lot.

He went into town and had lunch at the diner. Twice. He saw Rainie and Joyce both times, along with all the Stool Sitters. He also saw the Reverend Foley, Brandy from the post office, a very pregnant Annie Gatchell from the library, a couple former teachers, five former classmates, and Ruth.

He didn't once see the new doctor in town.

It was official, Zoe Parisi was avoiding him.

He didn't stop to wonder when that state of affairs had become unacceptable.

But the afternoon Matty Brennan Currick drove in and beeped her truck's horn in greeting he hadn't decided what—if anything—he was going to do about it.

He came out of the barn to see her reaching into the back seat of her pickup.

"Here, take this," she ordered, turning with an oversized pot with handles on each side. "I got carried away making stew, so I brought you some." She looked at him over the pot. "How are you doing?"

"Good. You can let go, Matty. I've got the pot. Thanks for bringing it, but—"

"Better take it inside before it gets cold. No wonder I was in the mood for stew with this crazy late spring. Go ahead, go in. You've got the heavy stuff. I've just got a little basket to bring in."

Not until he set the pot down on the stove did he turn around and see that the basket was moving.

"No. No way, Matty."

"You don't have to keep her. Not forever. Just for a little while until we sort out a home for her. Can you believe someone didn't want her?"

She took the squirm out of the basket and plunked a ball of fluff in his hands. It took both hands. And he had large hands.

"She's a collie and golden retriever mix—so *smart*. Well, you've met Sin, so you know how smart collies can be and the golden mixes in a good dose of laid back. And both breeds want to please their people, so you couldn't ask for a more trainable dog."

The puppy shifted around in his hold, making him worry he'd drop her. But she managed the maneuver without falling on her head and with little help from him.

"Not that you'll have to train her much. She's already housebroken and knows sit and stay and lie down. She's been great with the horses—though I'd keep her on a leash until you see how she does with the broncs and how they do with her. But you know how some dogs spook horses and other dogs are just perfect with them? Well, meet perfect."

The ball of fluff was goldy-red colored with white paws and white markings on the nose, forehead, ruff, and tail.

"Not that her name is perfect." Matty laughed and the ball of fluff's ears lifted. "We think she's about two and a half months old."

She might have kept talking. He wasn't sure.

The ball of fluff looked up at him with round, black eyes that seemed to ask questions and give answers all at the same time.

"Oh, *hell.*"

The ball of fluff wagged her tail.

"Unless you're going to fence around the house soon, I recommend a long leash—not retractable—that will give her some room but keep her of harm's way when you can't walk her." Matty was stowing cans of dog food in his fridge. "This is just until her tummy settles a bit. You can start mixing it with kibble—good kibble—soon."

He was at the table, finishing a bowl of stew she'd set there for him.

After tending the horses first thing this morning, he'd worked until after noon on his computer. He'd thought about lunch, but decided to check on just a couple things first. Hours had passed before Matty arrived.

The ball of fluff—he needed to get another name for this puppy—had kept Matty company in the kitchen a while and now was exploring the living room.

"You know, I'm not sure a pot of stew is enough payment for taking on a dog for its lifetime," he said, even though he'd come darned close to licking the plate.

"Hah. The dog's the real gift. The stew's just to keep your body and soul together until you realize it."

"I'm not in danger of wasting away."

"This fridge says otherwise. And you look thinner. Hmm."

"Are you looking for something?"

"I thought I might have left a dish here when we all came by."

"All the dishes are washed and in that end cabinet. Taylor and Val took theirs. I asked Dave to check, but he said he wouldn't dare try to guess which dishes might be yours."

She clicked her tongue. "All you have to do is read." She flipped one of the plates over, shot him a glance, and said, "This one's Ruth's." Another plate turned. "This is mine. And this last one—" She looked at the bottom. "—is Zoe's."

"Take it with you. Give it to her."

"No way. I have enough plates in my house already that I need to return. You're on your own when it comes to setting right whatever there is between you and Zoe."

"I don't know what—"

"Forget it, Halderman."

Just then the ball of fluff arrived at Matt's chair, sniffed at his boot, flopped down beside it, rested her chin on the toe with a deep sigh, and fell asleep from one breath to the next.

He knew he was grinning foolishly. He looked up to see that same expression on Matty's face.

"Or maybe not on your own," she said.

Zoe opened the door of her apartment and went instantly wary at the sight of him.

Before she could demand what had brought him up the steps to this narrow porch outside her second-floor door, however, she spotted his companion, stepped outside, dropped to her knees, and turned to mush.

Who said rodeo cowboys were stupid?

"Who's this?" she asked while cuddling the puppy, apparently to their mutual delight.

"This is my dog, Thunder."

She looked up. "Thunder."

"She'll grow into the name."

"*She?* You named a girl puppy Thunder?"

"Jarrod thought it went well with Midnight."

She laughed. At least her eyes did. Outside, she nodded and said, "That makes perfect sense."

He looked past her through the screen door to the desk with an open laptop and a quarter-eaten sandwich beside it. "Didn't mean to interrupt your lunch. Kind of late, isn't it?"

"Working on paperwork before I go back to the clinic for evening hours," she said absently.

"Came past the clinic. Your thermometer's rising."

"Not fast enough." She cut him a look, but didn't pursue that. "When did you get a puppy?"

"Matty—"

"Say no more. If my grandparents would let me, I'd have one of those rescue dogs in a second, probably a senior, who'd be happy to come along with me on house calls."

"What right do they have to tell you no if you want a dog?"

She looked up in surprise from Thunder, who had flopped over for a belly rub, in surprise.

Okay, maybe his tone had been harsh. It irked him somebody telling her she couldn't have what she wanted. Or anybody. *Anybody* being told by somebody else what to do. That was it. That's what bothered him.

"They own this building and rent out the apartments—the bigger one downstairs and this studio. They're my landlords, though they refuse to let me pay what I should for this place."

Now he felt like a fool. Landlords. Yeah, they did have a right.

"You need to get out of here so you can get a dog," he muttered.

"Someday." she said vaguely.

A sudden suspicion that bordered on certainty hit him that her apartment situation resembled her vehicle situation.

"How much money are you putting into the telemedicine fund? No, don't tell me, because I know it's so much that you're driving that old wreck and living where you can't have what you want."

She stood. "That's none of your business. Which raises the question—what *is* your business here?"

He'd blown all the goodwill Thunder had gained. Now he had to start from scratch. Might as well plunge in. "What are you doing Sunday?"

"That's—"

"None of my business, either. I know. And you're right. It's not." It clearly hadn't occurred to her that he might be asking her out. Not that he was.

But having the thought never cross her mind chopped him down to size.

She raised her eyebrows. "We agree, then. Now, I need to get back…"

"Tests come back on that hay you had checked?"

"Didn't Doc Johnson tell you?" From the suspicion in her eyes, she probably knew Doc had told him. But it was the first thing that came into his head when she'd been preparing to go in. "It came back positive for mold, just like we thought. Are you having any breathing issues? Any other symptoms?"

He frowned. "I'm fine. And I'm not here for a checkup."

"What *are* you here for?"

"I have your dish you left at my place."

She looked around pointedly.

"Left it in the car. But you might not want it right now. Thunder licked it." The puppy gave him a sorrowful look. Yeah, he was a liar. He cleared his throat. "I also thought you might like to come out to Pegasus Ranch. I'm going to have folks out to thank them for their help getting started. Everybody's said yes except Connor Malloy, but Jarrod's coming. And even though you'd rather I didn't run a horse hospice—"

"That's not fair. I—"

"And even though you're not partial to me, you might want to make an exception."

"Why?" It dripped with suspicion, but it was still better than no.

"Some friends are coming. I'd like you to meet them." And them to meet her. No, he wasn't saying that. Not to her. Not to them. Hell, he wasn't even saying it out loud to himself.

"That's very hospitable of you," she said coolly, "but I don't think—"

"Kalli and Walker Riley."

Her mouth had stayed open, starting to form her next word of refusal. Now it formed a perfect O.

He couldn't take his eyes off it. That mouth…

"Walker Riley?"

He looked away from her mouth. "Yup. Their kids and another friend, too."

"Well, I … Maybe for a short time… If there aren't any emergencies."

"Barring emergencies. They'll come in that morning and we'll have lunch."

"Can I bring something—"

That mouth… Bring that mouth…

"—if I can make it? But don't count on—"

Her phone gave off a ringtone of a muted police siren. Thunder jumped up and nosed at this enticing sound.

She answered immediately.

"Dr. Parisi. … Uh-huh… Jefferson hospital should be—… Okay. Yes. Okay. Kendall Road and Berring Ranch Road. Got it. On my way." She clicked off. Then apparently spoke to Thunder. "Accident. Have to go."

She reached inside, grabbed a jacket and her backpack, pulled the door closed after her, and gestured for him to go down the stairs.

"You go first. Thunder's slow on stairs. Don't want to hold you up."

She'd pulled out of sight before he and Thunder reached the ground. He strapped Thunder into the backseat harness Jarrod had informed him was the safest option, but when he slid behind the wheel, he didn't turn the engine on.

"Did you notice she hadn't eaten more than a couple bites of her lunch? It's past three. She's going to this accident, and then she has night clinic."

In the rearview mirror, he saw Thunder tipping her head, trying to make sense of his words.

"Yeah, I noticed that, too," he said. "And you're absolutely right. We should do something about that. Good thinking, Thunder."

CHAPTER NINETEEN

"What's he doing here?" Deputy Jessup demanded of no one in particular.

Zoe didn't bother to look to see what he meant. If there was something to be handled maybe he would finally do something useful instead of getting in the way.

She was occupied talking to Paul Afferson as the EMS guys efficiently secured him for the ambulance trip to the hospital in Jefferson.

Jessup strode up to the stretcher.

"I have another call. You'll have to do without me," he said importantly. He reached as if to pat her shoulder, she moved to the other side of the stretcher to check Paul's pulse. "I'll make sure onlookers don't intrude on your scene."

"Onlookers," muttered the head EMT as Jessup left. "One guy in a pickup. Why'd Jessup call you out at all, Dr. Z?"

She shrugged.

The EMT rolled his eyes. "Jessup had to know we'd be here first and we'd take the patient to Jefferson."

"You just don't like doctors messing up your workflow," she teased.

"You got that right with most docs, but you're welcome any time."

With the stretcher loaded, the head EMT asked her, "You going to follow us in?"

"No. I know Paul will get good care. And I've got to get back to the clinic in less than an hour. Just let me have a couple minutes with him."

"You have as long as it takes us to grab our gear. Then we're gone."

Paul Afferson, in discomfort from a broken collarbone, was primarily irked at himself. He'd swerved to avoid a deer, only to sideswipe a telephone pole.

"You're in good hands, Paul," she said as she climbed out. "I'll check in with the doctors in Jefferson to see how you're doing."

"We've got it from here, don't worry, Dr. Z." The EMT crew efficiently closed up, took their spots, and pulled out.

She slowly turned and advanced toward Matt Halderman, sitting on the tailgate of his truck parked well out of the way of the ambulance, her vehicle, or Paul's wrecked truck.

"Didn't take you for an accident junkie," she said dryly.

"I'm not."

"Then what is this about, showing up here?"

He hopped down from the tailgate and started for the truck's back door. "It's about you eating."

"What?" She wasn't sure she'd heard correctly with his voice muffled from his head being partway in the truck. But she did hear something else clearly enough to add, "What is that tune you keep humming?"

He emerged with Thunder under one arm and a diner bag in the opposite hand. Thunder's tail thumped at Zoe, though her nose was far more interested in the bag.

Matt had a guarded expression on his face. "Tune?"

"Yeah. You hum it a lot."

He gave a shrug she did not buy. "No idea. Have a seat. I recommend the tailgate. Though if you really want to sit on the ground…"

"No. But—"

He put Thunder in the truck bed, hooked netting from one side to the other as an improvised fence, then starting pulling things out of the bag.

He asked, "Unless you're not hungry?" But didn't stop his preparations.

"I'm starved."

He handed her something wrapped in paper. "Salami and chicken with lettuce, tomato, and pickle. Weird, but Rainie said it's the same as you ordered and didn't get a chance to eat."

"It's delicious. What did you get? Roast beef?"

"Of course."

"Not exactly original."

"Good's more important than original."

They chewed for a while in concentrated silence. He pulled out more containers. Potato salad, orange sections, and brownies. He must have asked Rainie what to get because he'd hit the jackpot.

"Why'd that deputy bring you all the way out here on this call when Jefferson's closer?" he asked.

She glanced at him, wondering if he'd heard the EMT. "Hard to know who's available sometimes."

He grunted. "Is there something going on between you two?"

"*No.*" Quickly, she tried to temper that appalled syllable. "I mean, Deputy Jessup is a dedicated officer and I admire that—"

"You can admire law enforcement and still see this guy's a jackass."

A denial just wouldn't come out of her mouth.

"And you don't like him touching you," Matt added.

"He doesn't mean… He's not very socially aware."

"I can make him aware that—"

"Absolutely not." That came out with no problem.

He didn't pursue it, instead saying, "You've got to make time to eat."

"It was an unusual day. Most days—"

"Go just like this. According to my sources," he added.

"Rainie? She doesn't know—"

"Not just Rainie. Polly was in the diner getting an early supper before the clinic's evening hours. She says you skip meals, don't get enough sleep, have no relaxation, and will soon be of no help to anybody."

Zoe slumped back a little. She'd heard those words many times from Polly. Somehow they sounded worse from him. "The clinic's under-staffed and—"

"Has been for years," he shot back.

"—if we could hire a couple PAs or NPs—"

"Pigs would fly."

"Hearing Polly coming out of you is like something from 'The Exorcist.' You're creeping me out."

He grinned. "Just relaying the message. So what are PAs and NPs?"

"Physician Assistants and Nurse Practitioners. We could use a couple of each. The PAs in order to offer more services and hours—"

"More hours? According to Polly you work all the hours of the day as it is."

"—at the clinic. And the NPs to extend home services, especially."

"You need all that even if you get your telemedicine program?"

"Even *when* we get the telemedicine program. Yes."

"But you already have some telemedicine stuff, right? Doc Johnson said you'd set something up for him."

"Singular, special events rather than an ongoing and diversified program. Plus, they have to each be set up and preparations made, clearing the connection, arranging our time—time we can't afford, as Polly keeps saying."

She'd said the last part hurriedly, expecting him to pounce on it to make his point again. Instead, he seemed distracted, absent-mindedly feeding Thunder tidbits of bread.

When he still said nothing, she finally asked, "What's that expression mean?"

He looked up. "Just something that's been kicking at the back of my head for a while and finally stepped up enough that I could catch it. Ever have one of those?"

"Sure. What's yours about?"

"This and that. Something Harold said to me. Harold Hopewell. The billionaire—"

"I know. Who changed your life."

Now an even stranger expression crossed his face.

"He helped. He definitely helped. He was a smart guy. Had learned a lot. Lost the love of his life, but didn't stop living. I respected him."

He wasn't lying, but he wasn't telling the whole truth, either.

She gathered her trash. He reached at the same time toward the corner of her sandwich she hadn't eaten, presumably for Thunder.

The back of his fingers brushed the side of her forearm. She froze, watching his large hand as it turned to lightly circle her wrist, then slid down to enclose her hand.

He lifted it slowly, starting to draw it to him.

That night…

Drawing her hand to his body… Bringing her to touch him as she so wanted to touch him… Telling her how he responded to her, to her touch…

She pulled her hand away, stood, stepping back.

"Thanks for the food. Bye, Thunder." She patted the dog from a safe distance. She didn't look at Matt. That, too, was safety. "I've got to go or I'll be late for the clinic."

That was her reason for leaving. Not because she was bizarrely jealous of a now-dead billionaire who'd been such good company to Matt for the rest of a night she'd thought had been theirs. Not because of a touch.

Delusional idiot.

No. No, she wouldn't be.

"Zoe."

She stopped. Reluctantly, she turned to him.

A man with a smile like that and holding a puppy should not be allowed.

"One o'clock Sunday?"

"Oh. Right. Okay. Barring—"

"Emergencies, I know."

"Yeah. You never said—do you want me to bring something?"

She had the most extraordinary impression of a fire surging hot and bright in him for an instant, then being strictly controlled.

"Salad or dessert, your choice."

Matt heard the powerful engine and came through the barn, wiping his hands.

As soon as the mammoth vehicle came to a stop, the passenger door popped open and young Jeff and Hayley Riley tumbled out, making a beeline for him. Hayley jumped into his arms and Jeff hugged him around the legs until he reached down and hoisted him up, too.

Walker and Kalli and their just-turned teen daughter Miranda emerged more slowly, while Gulch Miller climbed down from the driver's seat.

Matt whistled. "That's some horse trailer. Leaves the one you had at the rodeo grounds last summer in the dust."

Kalli clicked her tongue. "These things just keep growing and growing. Remember the first one, when Walker insisted I have a place to rest when I was pregnant with Miranda? That was perfectly serviceable, but he had to go and replace it with something fancier for each baby."

"Are you telling me—?"

"No," she said with a laugh. "Definitely no."

Walker grinned. "This time, we had to get a new one for Gulch."

"Don't you be putting this monster off on me, Walker," protested the older man.

Walker tipped his head closer to Matt as if imparting a secret, but said in his regular voice, "He loves the thing. Won't let me drive it."

"Not after that first time," Gulch grumbled. "Can't drive a vehicle like this like it's a da—darned tractor. And on top of that it took me forever to get the seat rigged right."

Walker's grin deepened. "Yeah, if I tried to drive his baby now, I'd have my knees in my mouth. He loves this one so much because he has his own quarters. Can't understand it, but the man wanted privacy. He used to share bunk beds with the kids."

"He snores," reported Jeff.

"Who snores?" Gulch demanded. "You sound like a freight train coming through a tunnel."

That set off giggles from several sources.

"Had to separate them," Kalli said. "It was like an unending slumber party with the four of them in those bunk beds."

"Well, it's time to get this monster set up so Gulch can get his beauty rest tonight, so let's get to it, you rug rats," Walker ordered. "You know the drill."

The kids sprinted toward the trailer, while the adults followed more slowly.

Kalli gave him a searching look. "How are you, Matt?"

"Good. Oh, you mean that allergic reaction? Steering clear of mold, but other than that…"

"That's good to hear. But there's something…" She looked him over. "Something else."

"Woman trouble," Gulch said flatly. The other three turned to him. "What? Think I don't recognize it? He's got the same look Walker had the summer you came back to Wyoming, Kalli. You might not have seen it, since you were having your own troubles."

"Man troubles," she murmured, with a smile at her husband.

" 'Spose that's only fair," Gulch said. "But that's what's all over Matt's face here."

Walker had said he wouldn't tell Kalli what he'd heard in the diner on his first trip to Knighton and from Matt's perspective Walker's expression was perfectly bland. Yet as Kalli turned to her husband now, her eyes narrowed slightly, it was as if she could read every word of that episode on his face.

Then she turned toward Matt with sharpened focus.

Slowly, she nodded. "I believe you're right, Gulch. As you so often are."

"Always said Kalli was the smartest of you lot," the older man said. They'd reached the trailer. "C'mon, let's get to work. We got to get these horses out, then set up."

Amid the activity of the next hour, Matt and Walker were alone just once—when Kalli discovered Thunder and called the kids and Gulch over to make her acquaintance.

"Did you… Uh, have you said something to Kalli?" Matt asked.

No need to specify what.

"Nope. Gulch neither. Not that it'll do you any good."

CHAPTER TWENTY

Zoe was late for the party Sunday, because Annie Gatchell's baby arrived early. Mother and baby had come through fine and were resting comfortably.

The doctor wasn't.

Having been up most of the night, there'd been no time or thought to prepare a salad or a dessert, but she did not arrive empty-handed.

"Need a hand?" Dave Currick called to her from the side porch, where tables and chairs were once again set up.

"Yes, please."

Dave, Jack, and Matt came down from the porch. Thunder, left behind, immediately started yipping and carrying on.

"I see you went for the essentials," Dave said as he pulled a flat of bottled water from the back of her vehicle.

"Can't ask for better." Jack took an equal amount of beer.

"Sorry, I didn't bring the dessert or salad," she said to Matt as he took the other flat of beer.

"No problem. Besides, Ruth covered both."

She looked up in surprise, spotting her grandparents now. She wasn't sure which surprised her more—that Matt had invited them or that Ruth had accepted.

She pulled the last batch of water out.

"Put that on here," Matt said, nodding to the beer he held.

"I can carry it."

"No need. Put it on here," he repeated. "Before my dog busts a vocal cord."

She acquiesced, partly for her ears and partly because she was tired.

She was careful not to touch him during the transfer. Maybe a little too careful, because she dropped the flat of water rather heavily on top of the beer. But he held on.

They followed Dave and Jack to coolers set on either side of the steps. They added to the drinks already cooling, then returned to the steps.

With Matt back on the porch, the yipping stopped and Thunder cavorted with delight.

He picked her up, trying to dodge licks aimed at his face.

"Zoe, I'd like you to meet my friends, Walker and Kalli Riley and Gulch Miller. There are three Riley kids out there somewhere, too." He gestured toward a band of kids apparently occupied with rolling down the side of the knoll. Jarrod Malloy was preparing to take the next roll.

Exchanging "It's a pleasure to meet yous" she shook hands with the short, gray-haired man identified as Gulch, then sophisticated yet relaxed Kalli, before turning to her childhood crush.

Her jaw nearly dropped to her toes.

Walker Riley was the man who'd been in the diner that day Joyce and Rainie had carried on so.

"Real nice to meet you, Zoe," he said in an easy drawl, giving no indication that he'd ever seen her before.

No, that wasn't quite true. There was a glint in his eyes. A glint of a shared secret just between them.

Between them and Kalli Riley, she realized in the next instant.

She must have said something appropriate back, because nobody gasped or laughed or paid any heed at all.

Except her grandmother, who ordered her to sit down, put a bottle of cold water in her hand, and set to filling a plate for her. "Because I know you didn't bother to eat."

"I'm sorry I'm late—" she started as soon as Ruth would let her.

"If delivering a baby isn't the best reason to be late, I don't know what is," Val said with a chuckle and a shared look with Jack. "Everybody's okay?"

"Perfect." Annie had said to spread the word, so she filled them in on the statistics.

"Now, you eat," Ruth ordered, presenting her a heaping plate. "And the rest of you stop hounding her with questions so she can."

"In the meantime, we'll fill you in," Matty said. "I hate it when I'm the last to arrive and everybody knows what's been talked about except me. So, let's see. We talked about kids. Walker and Kalli's amazing trailer. The before and after of Matt's house. Then, my husband, ever so tactfully, said Matt's barn looks like it's going to fall down. Matt said it could wait for repairs until fall."

Gulch snorted. "If that thing lasts to fall, I'll start playing the lottery, because it'll be a sure sign miracles are in season."

"That was the general attitude," Matty agreed. "So the guys decided they'd pitch in Thursday to make the most urgent repairs."

"Sorry I can't lend a hand," Walker said. "Rodeo keeps us tied to Park most of the summer, but come fall, we can be back for the rest of what that barn's going to need."

"But Jack and I hope you'll be here before that—for the wedding," Val said.

"And we're going to try," Kalli said.

"That about brings you up to date," Taylor said. "We were just talking about Thunder—honestly, how could you call that sweet girl Thunder?"

"Says the woman with a dog named Sin," Matt shot back.

"That was Cal's doing." The culprit grinned from his seat on the steps. "And it's short for Sincere, which fits him perfectly. How does Thunder fit that baby girl?"

"Her bark in my ear in the middle of the night."

"That's just a love song," Val said.

"Yeah, this one's always had a way with females." Gulch tipped his head toward Matt. Everyone chuckled. "I remember him as a beanpole, trying his charm on Kalli that first summer."

"Until Walker squashed me under his heel," Matt said.

Walker nodded confirmation. "Well-deserved."

"And then he started calling me ma'am, which at the time was something new for me." Kalli sighed. "Now it's an everyday occurrence."

Walker put his arm around her waist. "I'll call you darlin' for every ma'am you get." Their connection was strong and private for a moment, then Walker shifted the mood back. "And you'll be glad to hear Matt got his comeuppance. Heard him called Mr. Halderman, sir, when I was here before."

"Oh, I wish I'd heard that," Kalli said.

"And seen his face," Walker added. "That was the best part."

"Great to have old friends, isn't it?" Matt mused.

Walker clapped him on the back, a friendly gesture that might have felled another man.

"That it is, Matt. That it is."

The conversation and the food were plentiful and inviting.

The pinched look around Zoe's eyes eased as she ate and drank—only water, he noticed—and relaxed. She needed sleep, too, but this had helped.

He noticed she hadn't brought anything that involved a second plate he could hold hostage. That was okay. He still had the first one. He'd tucked it away, too, just in case she went looking for it.

She was laughing at something Gulch said when Matt sensed someone watching him. He turned slightly and met Ruth Moski's direct stare. Skidding away from that, he hit Kalli's thoughtful look.

He got up and headed for a cooler, asking if anyone else wanted something to drink. Most did. That occupied him for a while.

Kalli said, "Zoe, you weren't here when Matt showed us this amazing thing with Thunder. We can take a short walk and I can show you. That okay with you, Matt?"

Kalli didn't pitch her voice any louder when she said that last part, so Matt knew she assumed he'd been listening right along. He considered making a point of it, but since he *had* been listening that made his position a little shaky.

"As long as she's on the leash," he said.

Matt had been grateful this morning when Kalli hadn't pursued Gulch's declaration that he was having woman trouble. He knew from experience that if she set her mind to finding out what was in his head it was going to come out eventually.

Now, watching her walk away with Zoe, he would have gladly swapped a grilling this morning if it could have prevented this one-on-one conversation between these two women.

"Matt Halderman, I want a word with you."

Ruth had come up beside him as he piled new drinks into the cooler.

Suddenly Kalli and Zoe talking didn't seem the worst thing happening right now.

CHAPTER TWENTY-ONE

Ruth didn't beat around the bush. The second they were out of earshot of the porch-sitters, she said, "I know you took food out to Zoe the other day. Don't bother to deny it. I have it from two good sources."

He hadn't intended to deny it. "No need to thank me."

She snorted. It might have contained part of a truncated chuckle. "Well, I do thank you. But I'd thank you a lot more if she didn't look like she's been run over by a truck."

"I didn't—"

She interrupted before Matt had to figure out exactly what denial he'd planned to make. "Zoe works too hard. Always has. But it gets worse sometimes. First year of medical school was the worst I've ever seen her. She worked herself right into the ground and nearly beneath it. Going to medical school *and* working. Came down with pneumonia. But what really did her in was being heart sore from whatever you'd done to her right before the start of that school year. Because that's when she started doing her best to work herself to death."

"I didn't kn—"

She negated his words—or maybe her own—with a shake of her head that sent her feather earrings flying. "I'm not saying she intended to kill herself. Nothing like that. But she was taking all that unhappiness from whatever happened with you and pouring it into school and work. Pouring and pouring and pouring until she was in a hospital bed herself. Her momma couldn't go to her, not with three younger ones still at home and that useless second husband of hers."

"Second? Not Zoe's—"

"Zoe's father left when she was little. There one day. Walked out the next. Never came back. Sent a birthday card the first year and a letter to Brenda saying he'd started a new life, wished them well, and that was it."

Matt swallowed a curse.

"Brenda remarried, but he was no prize. Best thing she did was divorce him. Without him draining her purse every day, she started getting things straightened out. But that wasn't until the next year, the one after Zoe was so sick. By that time she was coming around and with Cal paying the rest of her way through school—"

"Cal?"

"Yeah. Likes to think nobody knows, so don't go blabbing. His family back East had money that he put into a foundation. It's done a lot of good around here. Not that he says it. Not Taylor, either. But you hear things."

"Why couldn't his foundation—"

"They're matching. But they can't fund the whole telemedicine program. A tax thing or something. It was looked into, believe me."

He believed her. It also scared the daylights out of him that she'd known exactly what he was going to say.

"And that's the other thing I know—what you're doing."

How on earth did she know that? Taking Zoe lunch, sure. There'd been Rainie and Polly to tell her. But he'd kept this to one other person—

"Doc Johnson and I go back a long way," Ruth said. "And he's seeing the same things in Zoe I am. I know my girl and what you're planning's not enough. I'm not saying it won't help something, but it's not enough. Not nearly enough to keep her from working herself into the ground again because of you."

"Hey, I—"

"Here's what I want to say to you. It took her a year and a bout of pneumonia to get past whatever happened with you the last time. And that was with you out of sight. With you digging in here like you might stay, heaven only knows what could happen. But whatever it is, a sandwich now and then isn't going to pass muster with me, young man."

Kalli held Thunder's leash as she led them in the direction of the knoll, with the delighted jabbering of the kids getting louder as they cut the distance.

Thunder covered at least twice as much territory as the humans by darting as far ahead as the leash allowed, running back, going sideways, jumping, and twirling. Then repeating.

Both women spent a lot of the walk laughing at the puppy.

In between, Kalli asked about Knighton, pointed out her kids, talked about how nice the people here were, and described how she and Walker helped run the well-known Park Rodeo, on the other side of the state.

Zoe started to relax.

"Here we are," Kalli announced to Zoe's surprise. Because "here" was the lane between the empty corral on their left and the pasture on their right. The only occupants of the pasture still appeared to be Python and Pizza.

"Watch this."

Kalli let the leash out so Thunder could get up next to the fence. The dog yipped excitedly.

Pizza paid no attention, but Python trotted toward them.

"Uh, Kalli…?"

"Shh. Just wait."

The ill-tempered horse came right up to the opposite side of the fence from the tail-wagging dog, put its nose down to puppy level and the pair snuffled at each other contentedly.

"That's amazing," Zoe said in a low voice.

Thunder gave a play bow and Python bobbed his head.

"I never would have believed it if I hadn't seen it. Of all the horses—"

That's when Kalli launched her surprise attack.

"Of course we've known Matt for ages," she said, as if Zoe had just asked about their friendship.

While Zoe mentally scrambled for a way to turn the conversation, Kalli continued.

"Showed up at the rodeo grounds the summer Walker and I came to help after Jeff's stroke—that's Baldwin Jeffries—"

Zoe nodded that she knew of the legendary founder of the Park Rodeo.

"—that was a difficult time. But it was the beginning of wonderful times." Kalli's smile bloomed. "And Matt was there. Young and so gung-ho about rodeo. He was a bronc rider to start, you know. It wasn't until that summer and seeing Walker on the bulls that he started riding them, too. He would study every move—the bulls' and Walker's.

"Now, knowing about his father's death and the situation with his mother it makes sense that he gravitated toward a man he wanted to emulate—a father figure. Back then it simply seemed like hero worship."

"He was fortunate to have found Walker Riley—and you, of course." With the older woman weaving her own history into what she was saying about Matt it would be rude to try to shut down this conversation. That was the only reason Zoe didn't.

They slowly started back toward the house, needing to encourage Thunder, who was reluctant to leave her friend.

"Thank you. It's mutual. Our kids adore him. Even at the start, he helped me understand Walker in ways I never would have on my own—sometimes you gain more insight into someone from other people around him, rather than direct from the source."

Zoe understood exactly what she was saying: Take my word for who Matt Halderman is because I know him and see him more clearly than you can.

Maybe.

Maybe not.

She might trust Kalli Evans Riley's judgment from here to the ends of the earth. She might believe every word the other woman said about Matt. But Kalli would never have the view of him that Zoe had because Kalli would never fall for him the way Zoe had—once had.

"You can be so close to something or someone that you need a bit of distance." Kalli laughed ruefully. "Though a divorce was rather more distance than either of us ever really wanted."

Zoe looked at her, surprised. "You and Walker were divorced?"

"Yes. We married very young, divorced very young. And it probably would have stayed that way if Walker and I hadn't both returned to Park to help Jeff and Mary Jeffries. Not that it was easy. That's where Matt helped. Seeing the fire in him as he started out in rodeo made me understand Walker better, even though I'd known him most of my life.

"I asked Matt once why he rode broncs and bulls when it so often meant getting hurt. Or at the least being frustrated, disappointed, broke. He told me about seeing a tornado as a kid at his grandparents' in Nebraska—his mother's parents. He tossed off that it was scary—" She smiled slightly. "—then focused on how fascinating it was to watch it go one way, then the other without knowing where it would go next. Unpredictable and powerful. He said he could feel that excitement under his skin. Something he never forgot. To him, that's what rodeo rough stock events felt like. Now, I'd be the first one down in the storm cellar, so I'd never see a tornado the way he described. But it opened a window for me to how Walker felt. And of course how Matt felt." Kalli glanced at her. "There's an old song about where love lives. Do you know it?" She hummed several bars.

"Oh." Zoe bit it off before blurting out that Matt kept humming that tune. But she had a feeling the woman knew what she'd been about to say anyway.

Kalli started to sing in a soft, pleasant voice, emphasizing lyrics explaining that servants and riches didn't create love, that, instead, love made simple things grand.

Zoe was smiling at the end. "I always liked that song. It reminds me of Knighton."

"I can see that. Maybe here Matt can finally learn where love lives. He hasn't truly believed in it—not for himself. Have you ever met his mother?"

The unexpected question threw Zoe off balance. Again. "I, uh, I knew who she was as a kid, but had more to do with his dad."

"That makes sense from what I've heard about Phil and what I know of Veronica. She not only thinks she's entitled to a certain lifestyle, she thinks Matt owes her. If I had my way, he'd never give her another penny. Oh, dear, now I've shocked you. Sorry. Walker says people miss my streak of fierceness. Thank heavens he likes it."

"When are you two going to rejoin us?" Walker called from the porch.

"Right this minute," Kalli said. "We were just talking about how amazing it is that Thunder's openness and love have reformed that grumpy old man Python."

"Unless Python's trying to lull Thunder until he has a chance to attack," Matt said darkly.

That drew a lot of scoffing, teasing comments. But what Zoe heard was Kalli saying, very low, "You don't recognize love when you see it."

CHAPTER TWENTY-TWO

With the sun rising Monday, Matt and Walker walked up the knoll under orders from Kalli, who was preparing the kids for departure and said she wanted them out of her way.

They reached the top in silence, looking west to where the morning sun touched the Big Horns' high eastern slopes into golden day.

"Lot of snowpack for this late," Walker said.

"The cold spring's holding it up there. Could be one of those seasons where it all melts at once. Or it might just hold through next winter."

Walker nodded. "I'd sure hoped you'd settle closer to us, but I see the draws. You've got a good place here with Pegasus Ranch. Suits your needs. And good people."

Matt knew the older man had spotted the roofline of the main house to their left. Walker shot him a look, but didn't mention the nearness of the house Matt had talked about getting back for years.

Matt was the one to keep the conversation going. "You and Kalli…"

"What about us?"

"I know you've been together a long time. But back at the beginning … did she make you feel … strange?" Walker gave Matt his whole attention. Matt regretted opening his mouth. "Never mi—"

"Strange how?"

"Never mind." Why on earth had he started this? "It's nothing—"

"Strange how?"

He wasn't going to get out of this by trying to ignore Walker. But maybe he could sidestep. "Strange like, not good. Not happy. Not—"

"You mean like your insides feel like you'd been riding a bull for eight hours instead of eight seconds?"

"Uh … I suppose."

"Still makes me feel that way."

Matt swore under his breath.

"Doesn't go away. Not if you're lucky." Walker gave a slow, private half grin. Then it faded. "Thing is, Matt, I'm not much good to you with this. I've known I loved Kalli since I was sixteen. If I'd been smart, I'd probably have known it when I was twelve. I don't know what it's like when you're a grown man and meet a woman who rocks you right down to your bones."

"Not sure I do either."

Walker raised his eyebrows, clearly doubting that Matt wasn't rocked down to his bones. "I mean I'm not sure I'm a grown man."

Walker grinned, then clapped him on the back. "Having that suspicion's a start, Matt. A darned good start."

"Maybe for me, but Zoe… There's something … something from the past."

Walker studied him. "Something separate from you? Or something you were part of?"

"Something… Something I did."

"Uh-huh." He squinted at the horizon for a few breaths. "That first summer at the Park Rodeo, I recall a conversation we had about a particular ride of mine."

Matt immediately knew what Walker meant, though he didn't see the connection. "Wasn't much of a conversation. You talked. I listened."

Walker slowly nodded. "Sounds about right. Interesting thing was a veteran cowboy had congratulated me on the good score."

"I don't remember that. Just Gulch, scowling like crazy."

"Yeah, well, Gulch wasn't congratulating me at all. He was telling me I was an ass when you came up all starry-eyed. Thing was, that veteran cowboy knew it was a great score but a stupid ride. Gulch only saw the stupid ride. Then there was you, seeing the ride and not realizing it was stupid."

"I did after our 'conversation' and you saying I'd never set foot in another rodeo if you ever caught me riding like that."

"What I didn't tell you, Matt, was I rode like a crazy fool that night because of fearing Kalli would walk out of my life a second time. First time, I'd gone wild and stupid. Made rides like that a lot. Did other foolish things. A lot of them.

"What I came around to realizing that summer we're talking about was that even if she walked out again I couldn't react the same way. Short way of saying it is I grew up. Thing is, I'm not saying that my changing was the reason she stayed then, stays now. Sure didn't hurt, I suppose. But what it comes down to was I couldn't change the past and I couldn't change how she felt. All I could change was me—what I did. Not just talk, but actions. Especially to Kalli."

Matt looked toward the beautifully untidy horizon of mountains. "I know I can't change what happened. Or how she feels about it."

"That talk going on in the diner … I got the feeling some folks are hard on Zoe for how she feels about the past. Maybe thinks she should let bygones be bygones soon as you said, 'Sorry, ma'am.' "

"They're idiots. She has cause. That's the truth of it. And if anybody says otherwise…"

Walker huffed out a breath, sparing Matt having to figure out a sufficient reaction. "Do you want her to trust you now?"

"I, uh, I don't know." That was the best he could do.

"That's something you're going to have to decide. Because healing up the distrust and working back to trust will take some doing if your Zoe's a smart woman. And I think she is."

"I know that."

"Glad you do. Say," Walker said in a different tone, "you know what I remember best about that whole conversation after that ride of mine?"

"Nope."

"You called me sir. Felt about a million years old."

"So that's what amused you so much about Jarrod calling me sir."

Walker set his legs wide and tipped his head back to the sun. "Felt good. Felt damned good to hear you pushed on my side of the 'sir' divide and see your face while you took the tumble."

They'd worked since early light this Thursday with few breaks. By mid-afternoon they sat on the porch steps surveying the barn. Matt distribut-ed water to his volunteer crew.

"Should stand a little longer now," Jack said.

"At least until tomorrow," Dave murmured.

Cal took the bottle Matt held out. "Thanks. New Internet service you're installing at the clinic sounds good. Now Taylor wants it for her office and for home."

"How'd you hear about—?"

"Polly told Rainie, who told Ruth, who told Taylor." He shrugged. "It's Knighton."

"Ruth told me to get it for the office. Soon," Dave said. "Matty can't be far behind. Everybody's real impressed."

"Not everybody," Matt muttered.

"Yeah, I wondered about that." Dave tipped his head back. "Saw Zoe dodge back into the clinic when she saw Matt coming down the sidewalk yesterday. They'd seemed to be getting along Sunday, so it seemed odd."

She'd certainly done an about-face yesterday afternoon. Matt could have gone without an outside observer confirming he'd been the cause of that effect.

"Just as well." As soon as he said it, he regretted it. He should have said something about Zoe only being nice Sunday because she'd wanted to meet Walker Riley. Too late.

"Why?" Cal asked.

Because of a touch.

Because it reminded me of what she wants to forget, and she saw that.

Matt said nothing.

Jack challenged him with, "Zoe's a great gal."

Dave, on the other hand, gave a slow nod. "Saw Ruth talking to you Sunday, Matt."

He didn't think Zoe needed her grandmother's encouragement to avoid him. But he wasn't telling these guys that.

"What's Ruth got to do with…?" Cal let that die out.

Dave's nod was more emphatic this time. "Yup. You've heard about mother tigers protecting their young? Try a grandmother tiger. Zoe's not just the apple of her eye, she's the whole fruit platter. When she was in med school and got so sick with pneumonia—Matt?"

"What?"

"You flinched."

"No, I didn't."

Dave looked at the others. "Definite flinch," Jack said. Cal nodded.

With that support, Dave asked with very little questioning in his tone, "You had something to do with Zoe getting sick back then?"

"How could I have—?"

"Give it up, Halderman. Matty's sure you knew each other before— and I don't mean as kids—and she's rarely wrong. If you're trying to shake loose of Zoe, we won't give you up to Ruth. Might think you're a damned idiot to dump her, but—"

"There's no dumping. Because there's nothing between us."

They all stared at him.

"I mean, there might be some … uh, interest. But one-sided, as you can tell, and it's not really… It's nothing."

Cal addressed the other two men. "I recall being a resident of that state of denial. Anybody else?"

Jack nodded. "Yup."

"It's not denial. There's nothing…"

"Do you want there to be something?" Jack asked.

"It's complicated, because—"

"Do you want there to be something?" he repeated.

"I… I, uh…"

"Don't need to tell us," Cal said. "But *you* should know."

Dave stood up and stretched. "Well, I think it's time."

"You're ready to get back to work?" Why didn't Matt feel as grateful as he should?

"Time we took you for a drive. To a place we know in Jefferson."

Jack looked blank. Cal made a sound that might have been a cough. Or not.

"There's no place in Jefferson I want to go." Matt said.

"It's for your own good," Dave said.

"The barn—"

"Will still be there when we get back. Probably. We're going now."

Cal stood. "C'mon, Matt. Once Dave's set his mind to something it's best to get it over with."

Matt looked at Jack. "Do you have any idea what this is about?"

"Not a clue. But since Dave's my boss…" He stood, too.

"Oh, hell." Matt rose slowly.

"That's the spirit," Dave said.

CHAPTER TWENTY-THREE

"Flower Power," Matt read aloud as they hustled him into a store across from the county courthouse in the center of Jefferson. "*Flower Power?* I thought you were taking me to a bar."

"At this hour? What do you take us for? Degenerates?" Dave seemed to be having a hard time not laughing.

"Hey." Jack sounded—and looked—like he couldn't decide if someone was pulling a fast one on him or if they'd just handed him a winning lottery ticket. "Hey."

"Yup," Cal said, apparently to Jack. Though Matt had no clue what he was yupping about.

"What's going on?" He asked as the loamy scent of plants hit him. "What the hell is this place?"

"What's it look like?" Dave asked.

"Some kind of florist or something."

"Or something," Cal muttered.

Before Matt could zero in on Cal to demand an explanation, a woman's voice said, "Hello, gentlemen."

A hand at his back propelled Matt through foliage growing up, down, and sideways from plants stuck into containers he'd never expected to hold plants, including what he'd swear was an old bedpan and an antique boot. His hip hit a counter and he looked up to see a woman wearing a green apron that said "Delicate Flowers Have Great Powers."

"What can we help you with today here at Flower Power, where the power of—Oh!"

For an instant Matt thought she'd reacted to him. But no, she was looking past him. At Jack.

"*Mimulus guttatus.* Yellow monkeyflower," she said, nodding to herself.

Matt turned, expecting Jack to be as lost as he was. Instead, he tipped his hat and said, "Ma'am," with a strange smile.

"And you—" She pointed at Cal. "—fireweed."

"Yes, ma'am."

"Remember me?" Dave asked.

"Of course. Indian paintbrush. In a wedding bouquet." She shook her head, but smiled. "So strange, but quite appropriate. It's been a number of years, but I'd never forget that. Oh, but where's bur marigold? He said you'd sent him."

"I did. He's in New York City with my sister, who's now his wife. They live there with their family."

"Ah." The woman's apparent pleasure extended the syllable. "How lovely. Of course you married with the Indian paintbrush bouquet. And you?" She looked at Cal.

"Yes, ma'am. Married, two kids."

"And this one's next." Dave clapped Jack on the shoulder. "Getting married later this year."

Matt had an uneasy feeling. That scratch between his shoulder blades he used to get when a particularly frisky bull eyed him like a toy it intended to trash.

"What is going on?"

No one paid him any heed.

"How delightful," the woman said, beaming at them all. "Now, what can I do for you?"

"It's what you can do for him." Dave's hand at Matt's back pushed him forward again and only then did he realize he'd been backing up. "Matt, tell her about Zoe."

"What?"

"She's a doctor. Helps people all the time," Cal said.

"I don't think that's how it works," Dave said. "Tell her about your relationship."

"We don't have—"

"They had something a while back but he messed it up," Jack offered.

"Hey. That's—"

"And now she's avoiding him," Dave added. "Tell her more stuff, Matt."

"This is crazy. No offense, ma'am, but… No way."

He might have been too emphatic, maybe even owed the woman more of an apology—though not enough to follow Dave's crazy order—but then he realized she wasn't paying any attention to him.

Not to him or anything else, in fact, judging by her unfocused stare.

"Nothing in here, I think. But… Oh. Yes, definitely… So many possible paths…" She blinked, looked at him, and commanded, "Come with me."

She turned and started into a room beyond the counter.

Matt didn't move. The others boxed him in, and started him forward by simply walking. He could fight to break free…

Fight to break free? Talk about an overreaction. Besides, he wasn't about to burn bridges with these men who were his neighbors, not to mention free labor.

He'd go along for now and let this craziness play itself out.

They followed the woman out the back of the shop and into a garden. Barely single-file paths divided raised beds with lines of plants in every bed. It was like an army of plants on parade.

"He's got to choose from all these?" Jack asked.

"I don't know how to choose a flower—"

The woman interrupted Matt by taking hold of his sleeve and tugging him along behind her. "The wildflower—the right wildflower—will choose you."

This was getting weirder and weirder.

"Though I do have a general idea, so… Yes. Something in this bed."

At least the plants in the bed she indicated weren't just seedlings, but had flowers starting to show.

"Go on," the woman said.

"Uh, that one I guess." He pointed, just to get it over with.

"Ah. Threadleaf Phacelia. Interesting. Very interesting."

The name sounded familiar, but he was focused on the way she'd said "interesting." He didn't like it. Didn't like it at all. Didn't like the way the others looked at him, either. Like a specimen in a lab. The woman bustled over to get a pot. She carefully dug around the plant and placed it in the pot, settling soil around it with gentle fingers.

And then he realized why the name sounded familiar.

The flower he'd picked was the same as the one they'd seen blooming on the knoll that first day Zoe came to Pegasus Ranch. The one he'd said was a weed and she'd said was a wildflower.

He picked it because it was familiar from that day. That's all. No big mystery.

"Isn't that blue weed?" he asked.

"It is *not*." She was even more indignant than Zoe had been. "*Phacelia linearis*, commonly known as threadleaf or linear leaf phacelia, is a native wildflower across much of our western half of this continent. Blue weed is invasive and not a native."

"What's interesting about this threadleaf flower?" Cal asked.

Matt frowned at him. He didn't seem to notice.

"It blooms in the spring, as you see—April to June mostly. It's quite lovely with its open, welcoming blossom in shades of lavender to blue. Which," she said with a severe look toward Matt, "some ignorantly mistake for blue weed when all they have to do is open their eyes and recognize what's in front of them. In addition, it is drought tolerant, which certainly is a benefit in Wyoming. Gardeners are increasingly using it in wildscaping."

"Wildscaping?" Jack repeated.

"Landscaping to provide healthy habitat for our wildlife, including birds and butterflies. Wildscapes particularly rely on native plants, so they not only provide better habitat, but also conserve water. Threadleaf phacelia takes good care of all the creatures, don't you?"

She was talking to a plant. She might be a nice woman, but when it came to hobbyhorses she was a champion rider.

"And since *phacelia linearis* can not only go for long periods without water, but is also nearly free of pests or diseases, it is eminently suited to that purpose. It accepts full sun to partial shade, so it's adaptable. Being a native plant is a bonus. As is its history."

"Ah," Dave said, as if they'd reached the point he'd been waiting for. "Lewis and Clark found it?"

"Meriwether Lewis collected it during their expedition, yes, but he certainly wasn't the first to find it. Indian tribes used it for many purposes, including making a tea to treat colds and fevers."

The other three men looking at him at the mention of fever.

"Several tribes have considered it beneficial for a general sense of well-being," the woman added.

"Kind of like a doctor," Cal murmured.

"I can see how you would say that," the woman said. "Threadleaf phacelia is also a deceiving plant."

"Deceiving?" That came out sounding angry. Matt cleared his throat. "How can a plant be deceiving?"

"Its flowers look so delicate, yet it is a very strong plant. Indeed, some call varieties scorpion weed, both for the curves of its petals and for a rash it can induce. Yes, indeed," she said cheerfully as she finished fixing the pot, "it can start an itch that's impossible to get rid of. Now, there are a number of other interesting points..."

CHAPTER TWENTY-FOUR

Riding in the back of Dave's truck with the plant on the floor between his boots so it wouldn't tip over, Matt kept hearing the woman's words about an itch impossible to get rid of.

"What'd she call that plant again?" Jack asked.

"Scorpion weed," he said.

"No, the other name."

"Fa—Celia," Dave said. "Like the note in the scale and then the girl's name."

Jack turned from the front seat to look at him. "That's the one Zoe talked about. She said it was like a woman's name, like fa-Clara. But Ruth knew the name. Right?"

"Yeah."

"Should be fa-Zoe," Cal said. The others chuckled.

Matt remained silent. This had been one of the stranger afternoons he'd ever spent.

"How'd you guys know about this place?"

"Stumbled on it because it's across from the courthouse. Matty needed a wedding bouquet when we got married and she wasn't exactly in to wedding planning," Dave said. "After that … it's been the right place a few times when somebody needed something."

Since he was the only somebody who'd bought something that did not soothe Matt's uneasiness.

"Those photos of the wildflowers Val took… How'd you guys know so much about them?"

There was a momentary silence. "Can't help but pick up things here and there," Cal said casually.

"What're you humming?" Val asked Zoe.

Zoe had stopped at the Slash-C to see more of Val's photographs around noon Friday on her way back from checking on a patient west of the Curricks' ranch.

She'd selected six photos for Val to enlarge and have framed for the clinic. They were putting back the others when Val asked the question.

"An old song," Zoe said.

An old song that had become the earworm to end all earworms thanks to Kalli Evans Walker and Matt. Zoe woke up to the song in her head and went to sleep with it in her head. As for her dreams… Nope. Wasn't going to think about those.

"Now, about delivery, Val. Don't worry—"

"I'll have them next week. What's the name of the song? I like that tune."

"It's, uh, I think it's called 'Where Love Lives.' That's part of the lyrics, anyway."

Val shot her a look, but instead of asking more questions, she pulled out her phone, tapped away, and soon they were listening to Hal Ketchum's yearning voice.

Great, now she'd have his voice in her head as well as Kalli's and Matt's hum.

"I like that," Val said at the end. "And it's perfect for you and Matt."

"What? No. There's no—"

"Sure there is. He encountered that other kind of life—his success in rodeo and business—but now he's come here, because this is where love truly lives. You."

"I had nothing to do with his coming here. *Nothing.* He was as horrified as I was—" Recognizing the cliff at the end of that sentence, she bit that off.

"I *knew* it. I had a feeling from Beautify Knighton Day that there's a tie between you."

"No, no tie. Matty got a wrong impression and—"

"Matty never mentioned anything. And tie isn't quite right. Unless it's frayed some. Chemistry? Yeah, but not the usual kind. More complicated. Maybe—"

"You're forgetting that *you're* the one he flirted with." Zoe produced a credible chuckle.

Val's wave dismissed that. "Nervous tic."

"Nervous? Matt Halderman?"

"Sure. When women feel shy, they clam up, try to fade into the woodwork, or maybe get real formal—my cousin used to do all three before she met her husband. Well, she'll still start sometimes, but he gives her this look, and she shakes it off. Anyway, that's how most women react. But men are told they can't be wallflowers—especially a man like Matt—so they laugh too much or make bad jokes or get drunk or automatically flirt."

Could she be right? There had been times he'd talked about his horses, his app, his business like they were a lifeline.

"But I wouldn't say it was shyness with Matt," Val added. "More like he's wary of women and that's his defense mechanism."

"Matt Halderman? Wary of women?" Her laugh had an edge. "What does he have to be wary of?"

"Same as everybody else. Getting hurt."

Him getting hurt?

Zoe kept her interest mild. "You said especially a man like Matt. Because he rodeoed?" Rodeo cowboys, especially ones who looked like Matt, were often pursued.

"No, I was thinking of things I've heard about his mother. You start to see a pattern. But if I've said too much…"

Zoe should grab this opportunity to stop this. Right now. "What pattern?"

"If you promise you'll treat this like patient-doctor confidentiality…"

She nodded.

"It's pieces of comments, a phrase, a tone, a look. I bet most aren't even aware of it. But sometimes an outsider like me can put the pieces together better than folks who have too much information. You know?"

Again, Zoe nodded. She'd seen that in medicine. Fresh eyes, a new perspective could spot what others were too close to see.

Just as Kalli had said.

"The snippets about Matt's mother say she's a pretty, charming woman who is selfish and used to getting her way. Even when people think they're complimenting her that's what comes through."

Doc Johnson describing a little boy with scarlet fever.

Kalli's words about Veronica Halderman.

Matt's emphasis when he'd said of the inheritance, *Nobody's getting their hands on it.*

And earlier, what he'd told her that night at the B&B…

She sold it. He was hardly in the ground and she just sold the ranch that had been in our family for generations.

"I… I think you're right." Zoe looked up quickly. "That's doctor-patient confidentiality."

"Sure thing."

"But his dad was a great guy. He was helping someone change a flat tire when he died. That's the sort of person he was."

"He'd have to be, wouldn't he?" Val asked. "The kind of person Matt's mom sounds like isn't going to choose a mate who *doesn't* give. And give and give and give. I had a boss—a chef—and everything revolved around him. Not just the kitchen and the restaurant. I'm talking the moon and the sun and the entire planetary system. His wife is this terrific woman who gives and gives and gives, because she agrees with him—the universe revolves around him. Made me want to tear my hair out. Couldn't she see he was taking advantage of her? Nope. To her, it was the way things should be.

"That's probably how Matt saw things growing up, too—that how his mom and dad interacted was how things should be. But his dad dying and his mother selling the ranch jolted him out of that track."

"Of course that would be hard on any kid, but—"

Val shook her head, then contradicted that by saying, "Hard on him, yes. But it might have saved him from falling for the same kind of woman his father did. They say people repeat their parents' relation-ships—thank heavens mine are relatively sane and love each other madly. I suppose Matt could have turned out to be as self-centered as his mother, but that doesn't seem likely with this horse hospice… Wait a minute. Maybe he *is* taking after his dad. He's taking care of creatures who aren't giving back."

Zoe felt buffeted and unsettled. "I… I, uh, I should go."

"Sure, sure. God, Zoe, you look shell shocked. Sorry my mouth got away from me and—"

"No. No, really, Val. I appreciate what you've said. It… it might help me understand a patient. And that's always good."

Val pulled her into a hug. "Yeah, right. A patient."

CHAPTER TWENTY-FIVE

Zoe was humming that tune again as she entered the side door of the clinic and went to the office.

She stopped humming at the sight of a female butt protruding from under Doc Johnson's desk.

"Got you, you little devil," a voice that presumably went with the derriere said.

"Excuse me? What are you doing?" The form backed out quickly from under the desk and straightened. Zoe blinked at a head of coppery curls. "Who are you?"

"Oh, hi. You must be Zoe. I'm Chris, Matt's IT guy."

"Matt's IT *guy*?" This curvaceous woman with the wild hair was the person who'd spent two nights at Pegasus Ranch according to the Knighton grapevine?

"Uh, yeah. It's easier to say it that way. IT person sounds so stuffy."

"What is Matt Halderman's IT *guy* doing in my office?"

"Hooking you up to faster and more secure service. What you had is—"

Polly hustled. "Zoe. Dr. Parisi. You're not supposed to be here."

"Why not?"

"You're supposed to be at the Slash-C."

Zoe waved that off. "What is going on here?"

Polly looked at Chris, who looked back at her. "You'll have to ask Matt."

Chris looked from Polly to her. "Yeah, you have to ask Matt."

Matt came out of the barn when she tooted the horn. He looked wary. Had he seen her duck away in town the other day? Had Polly or Chris called after she'd left the clinic?

"Matt, I want to talk to you."

"Okay."

"I met Chris."

"How'd that happen?" So apparently neither Polly nor Chris had called.

"What do you mean how'd that happen? I walked into my office and she was under Doc Johnson's desk."

He frowned. "Polly thought you'd have lunch at the Slash-C."

"They invited me, but—"

"So you haven't eaten lunch? Again."

"That is not the point."

"It's my point. We're eating lunch before you launch into whatever's brought you out here under a full head of steam."

"I am not—"

"Not another word." He strode toward the house.

She raised her arms, let them flop to her sides. Fine. She might as well eat.

She started up the porch steps then stopped, and backtracked down two. Her eyes had not deceived her. "What's this?"

He was at the door. "What's it look like?"

"That wildflower we saw over on the knoll. Fa-something."

"Phacelia."

She'd take his word for it. "You transplanted it here?"

"No. I bought a pot of it and planted it."

"You bought—I thought you didn't like it."

He got a strange look in his eyes. "A man can change his mind, can't he? Change his opinion based on new information. Better information."

"Like what information?"

"Uh. They call it scorpion weed."

"That's why you changed your mind about it?"

"Maybe. Some species get prickly." He gave her a pointed look.

"They can cause an itch. But you can tell this kind—threadleaf phacelia—because it's got a bigger corolla. That's all the petals of the flower taken together."

"Where'd you learn all this?"

"Oh, you know. You pick things up, like I told you before."

"You were talking about being on the rodeo circuit then. You learned about threadleaf phacelia and corolla on the rodeo circuit?"

He shifted his weight. "Not exactly. Point is, it's pretty. Pretty in places you wouldn't expect a whole lot of pretty. Grows where it's dry, where the showy, tender ones shrivel up. Rocky areas where you wouldn't think anything but sagebrush could grow. Scrub where it seems like the only pretty is the sky up above."

Her lips parted, but she couldn't think of a thing to say.

"It's practical, too. Indians used it for medicine," he said.

She looked at the plant again. "I never heard that."

"Made tea out of the roots and gave to folks to help colds. Treated fevers, too. And one tribe used it for just about any kind of feeling bad—sort of like going to the doctor all in one plant."

Boy, she must need food, because this conversation was not making sense.

"Let's go in," he said.

She followed him in, still shaking her head as he pulled out sandwich makings, setting them on the counter.

Impulsively, she asked, "Did your mom used to make you sandwiches?"

"Nope." He pulled out plates and handed her a knife.

"Did she do things with you? Play or—?"

"What I remember is being around the ranch, being with Dad on horseback, in a truck, on a tractor. Only thing she ever did connected to the ranch was sell it."

"Your dad must have loved her."

He looked up, surprise showing. "I suppose so."

"And she loved your dad and you. Loves you."

He returned to his sandwich-making. "She loves my bank account."

"Matt, she's your mother."

"Doesn't change that she's shallow and self-centered." He said that with no heat. "First time she ever came to see me ride, she wanted a hundred thousand dollars. For a vacation in Europe."

Zoe pulled in a breath.

"Wasn't the last time, though she stopped coming when she realized I wasn't earning as much. Then, when the business took off, suddenly I'm getting visits from dear ol' Mom. But don't worry, Ms. Take Care of Everybody, I put money in an account every month. She knows nothing about it or it would be sucked dry tomorrow, if not today. But I know I'll be supporting her in her old age—and that husband of hers, too, probably—so I needed to start early."

"I... I don't know what to say."

"Nothing to say." He looked over at her sandwich. "Really? No mustard?

"I don't care for mustard. Not since I changed my baby brother's diapers."

He froze with a knife loaded with mustard poised over the bread. "That's dirty pool."

She laughed.

He looked from her to the bread. "Nope. I still like mustard."

She laughed harder as he spread it on thick.

"You came out here to talk about my mother and flowers?"

"No." She set her plate on the table and sat. "I want to ask you—"

"Oh, no. We eat. Then we talk."

CHAPTER TWENTY-SIX

He watched her wipe her mouth with the piece of paper towel serving as a napkin—*that mouth*—brush her hands over the plate, then lean her elbows on the table and rest her chin on her steepled hands.

"Okay, talk, Halderman. The woman I saw in the clinic office, who said her name is Chris?"

He nodded.

"Is your IT *guy?* The same one you had staying here?"

"She slept in the bed." Zoe blinked, and he quickly added, "I was on the couch. When she was staying here, I mean. For this trip, Doc got her a room in town."

"That's not the point—and none of my business. What was she doing in the clinic office that neither she nor Polly would tell me about?"

While she'd been asking about his mother—where had that come from?—he'd had time to think about this. Any thought of it being a surprise was gone. Might as well spill it.

"Your connection at the clinic is crap. Chris is fixing that."

She frowned. "You don't need to do this, Matt. I told you, I understand that you made Harold Hopewell a promise."

He shifted in the chair.

"This was something I could do, Zoe. My business has the resources and the know-how. So I did it—or Chris is doing it."

She looked at her hands. "It's kind of you, but—"

"I know that thermometer in front of the clinic's not filling as fast as you'd like. But whether you reach the goal or not, Doc Johnson said you'd had trouble with teleconferencing you've tried. This will fix that.

There was no way you could support a telemedicine program if—when—you get it with the system you had. Would you question a donation or help from anybody else?"

She stood, took her plate and glass to the sink and rinsed them. Came back to the table and picked up her keys.

Finally she looked at him. Studied him with those eyes he hadn't been able to forget.

It wasn't the shape of them or the color. It was what was behind them.

"You're right. On behalf of the clinic and our patients, thank you."

He stood. "That isn't what—"

She was already heading out. He followed her to the porch, picking up his work gloves from beside the door with one hand, while the other circled her arm to keep her from going down the stairs.

"Zoe. If I hadn't left that night—" He had no idea where that came from.

"But you did. We can't undo what's done."

He slapped the gloves against the side of his thigh, a puff of dust spurted out. "That's right. You're right. No use wondering what if. Only dealing with what is. But there's something… Something I should have said. I'm sorry you were hurt, Zoe."

Her muscles went taut under his hand. But her voice was calm and even. "And now I say there's nothing to be sorry about? Is that what you expect?"

Was this what Walker had heard those women talking about in the diner? *She was on at Zoe about how she should forgive you everything. Or maybe it was anything.*

"No. I don't expect that."

"Some women might fall at your feet and froth because you said you're sorry—"

"I can't see you falling at anyone's feet, and you'd give me a medical reason for any frothing."

She stared at him three beats, then released a long breath that eased her shoulders and jaw. "I didn't mean to snap at you."

"But," he prodded.

"But there's this thing," she said, then stalled.

"What thing?"

"This thing with women—some women. They think if the man says something and the woman doesn't accept it at face value right then and there or withholds judgment to see how things play out, it makes the woman a bitch."

He frowned. "Women think that about other women? Why?"

"I have no idea. But I've seen and heard it. Too often. Working with women in ERs, clinics, shelters." She pushed her hair back with her free hand. "There'd be group sessions and time after time some women would say they'd had to show their love by having faith in the man— faith that he would live up to what he said. Trusting his word without any proof and despite evidence to the contrary."

"You have no reason to trust me." She started to turn. "No. I don't mean—I'm not asking you to trust me despite having no reason to. I'm saying I know why you *don't*. Trust's based on experience. And your experience with me… That night… When I woke up and looked down at you, as innocent as innocent could be—"

"I wasn't a—"

"Had nothing to do with that. It was… Me." He swallowed. "Rodeo had done fine for me, but I was starting on the downhill. And then what? I hadn't squandered my winnings, thanks to Walker and Kalli chewing my tail. But what was I going to do? Not ranch, not after—I'd bought a couple B&Bs just so I had somewhere to hang my hat, but was I going to run one? Hell, no. Ever since my mother sold the H Bar H, I'd been on the move—away from her, away from her jerk of a husband, away from what she'd done, who they were. I just kept moving and moving, but not getting anywhere. I was a beat up rodeo cowboy with no future, no direction. I looked in that bathroom mirror and saw all that. Then I started to go back to that bed and to you."

Sleeping with one arm across the space he'd left when he got up, as if embracing where he'd been.

"You. Aching to do all this good in the world. Plans and goals and the determination to make every damned one of them come true. And there was me, not one goal in the world. I saw what I was and I saw what I'd done."

"What you'd done," she echoed blankly.

"I'd seduced you."

Her mouth opened, but she said nothing.

"You know how long it took for me to decide I wanted you? Half a second, less. The sight of you standing there in that bathroom doorway, that's all it took… And then I set to making it happen. You didn't have a chance. I didn't remember you, Zoe. Not even when you told me who you were. I didn't really remember you until I was talking with Harold in that diner and something he said… Anyway, *that*'s when I remembered from when you were a kid. After I'd taken you to bed. After I seduced you."

Her mouth closed.

Then it opened again.

"*You* seduced *me*?" Laughter was in her eyes and voice. "Oh, Matt. The instant you opened that bedroom door I was ready to climb all over you. I'd've probably dragged you to that bed if you hadn't led me there."

More than a few times in his life Matt had experienced the sky and arena dirt swapping places in a heartbeat when a bronc or a bull threw him.

But this time he wasn't moving. So it had to be the world that had just flipped.

His mouth worked, but no words came out. He shook his head. And kept shaking it until he produced, "No way."

"If you did any seducing, Matt, it happened when you were twelve and I was nine and you walked the fence at the H Bar H and I thought you were the greatest thing that had ever lived."

She touched his cheek. He reached up and caught her hand to keep it there before she could withdraw it. Quick reactions came in handy.

His mind wasn't reacting as fast, though. "You were there that day?"

"I was. And I was in awe."

"Nothing to be in awe of. I didn't get very far. I fell off and did something to my arm."

"Bone bruise."

"How do you know…? Oh, my records—"

"No, I knew it then. I heard Doc Johnson tell your dad. Then I went to the library and looked it up. I wanted to know how to cure someone of a bone bruise, how to take away the pain. That's…"

She partially turned, but he still held her hand to his cheek. "That's what, Zoe?"

"That's what started me on wanting to be a doctor."

To cure him. To take away his pain.

"Zoe."

He cupped the back of her head with his free hand, still keeping his other over hers against his stubbled cheek, and he kissed her.

It jolted through him. Just the way it had that night.

He'd thought he'd made up that sensation, convinced himself it couldn't be real. It was. And it was stronger…

She kissed him back.

She parted her lips. They deepened the kiss together, angling to meet each other fully.

Turning, he pressed against her, bringing her back against the house, feeling that sweetness of her body against his.

He knew it. Remembered it. How could it be so right, so fresh? He knew how they would fit. How it would feel to enter her, to bring her to a climax that shuddered through her and into him.

He knew all that.

He wanted it. He wanted her.

Then her hand pressed against his chest.

Not hard. But there.

Not holding on to him, not inviting more. Not taking them where he knew they could go.

He tightened his hand in her hair an instant, not pulling, just enough to imprint the sensation of those strands.

Then he let go.

Both hands, stepping back.

Her hand slid along his cheek before dropping to her side.

"I… I have to go," she said.

At the bottom of the steps she turned back. "Matt, I'm sorry you've felt bad about how things started that night. You have no reason to apologize. I mean it. At the very least I was a full and willing partner. And I've never regretted that.

"It was the best night of my life. The night when I opened up and talked to someone about what I wanted to do and why I needed to do it, and how hard it was to do and how wonderful. The night when I opened up … sexually. The night when I—" She paused. "—loved."

"Zoe—" He surged forward.

She held up a hand, freezing him in place at the top of the steps.

"It wasn't that or how it started that bothered me. It was the end… The end of a one-night stand."

Air streamed out of him like he'd been gut punched. "I did that."

"No. I did it, Matt. Because in my own way I did what I was saying those other women did. I took that leap with no thought to how it might feel to fall."

CHAPTER TWENTY-SEVEN

She drove out of sight, then pulled over, still on the ranch road. She was shaking too much to be safe on the highway. Her hands, her arms, her knees, her feet, her heart. All shaking.

She rested her head against the top of the big old steering wheel, trying to breathe.

A kiss. One kiss… Okay a series of kisses, but still… And she was a shaking mess. If he'd taken one step toward the bedroom would she have followed?

Possibly.

Probably.

But he hadn't. And she'd grabbed on to some sense and ended it.

Because she was no longer that kid looking up at the boy so carefree and daring, who caught the rays of the sun until he glowed with it… She wasn't. She couldn't be.

You might think you've learned your lesson, moved on, gotten over. And then here comes that same lesson banging away at your heart and head with fists wearing spiked gloves.

She hadn't paid a physical price as too many other women had, but she'd been foolish by leaping emotionally that night, all based on a childish crush, a fantasy.

And in doing so, she'd been utterly and completely unfair to Matt.

She'd never paused that night to consider how he felt. And then she'd blamed him for not feeling the same way she had.

How had she never recognized that before?

"Hey, Doc Z."

She jumped and turned to see Jarrod, accompanied by Midnight, of course, just outside her open window.

"You okay, Doc Z?"

"I'm fine. Fine. Jarrod."

He frowned. "You look kind of splotchy. Are you coming down with something?"

Just a recurrence of a major case of Matt Halderman that she'd hoped had gone into remission.

She stifled the urge to laugh hysterically. That wouldn't do much for the patient's confidence in his doctor.

"I'm a little tired," she said, needing to tell him something.

"Mom gets like that, too. A lot lately." Maybe he was satisfied to pack her behavior away into a box labeled "The Strangeness of Grown-Up Women," because he didn't seem inclined to explore that any further. "Were you coming up to the home ranch?"

"No. Why? Do you need me to?"

"Not for me. I'm good."

His breathing sounded great, his color was good, but there was something bothering him. What—?

He interrupted her thoughts. "But if you're not coming up to the home ranch why're you here?"

She looked around for the first time and realized she had pulled over where the ranch road dipped down into a long-dry creek bed.

And then it hit her. She'd pulled away from Matt's house in such a tizzy, she'd turned the wrong way on the ranch road and was headed away from the highway instead of toward it.

"Well, I'm glad to have run into you, Jarrod. To check in on you. You doing okay? Any more episodes?"

He backed up from her vehicle. "No. I'm good. No problems. Haven't used the inhaler once. No need for a checkup or anything."

Way to distract from your own muddleheadedness—obliquely threaten a kid with a checkup.

"I'm glad to hear that, Jarrod. Guess if I'm not needed here then I'll be on my way."

Need.

Yeah, that was something she wouldn't think about while she was behind the wheel.

Thunder roused Matt by crying for her dinner. Otherwise he might have sat on the porch step all night, listening to the voice in his head.

Funny thing was, it wasn't Zoe's voice.

It was her grandmother's. Talking about Zoe's father leaving.

He'd started a new life, wished them well, and that was it.

There one day. Walked out the next. Never came back.

Change one word, just one word, and it was what he'd done to Zoe.

There one minute. Walked out the next. Never came back.

He couldn't have given her what she deserved, but he could have done better than that.

God knows he should have done better than that.

The next evening, Zoe returned to her apartment after a long day to find Matty Currick and a wrapped package outside her door.

She trudged up the stairs.

"Tough day?" Matty asked.

"Yeah."

"The fund-raising?"

"At the rate we're going, we're not going to make it."

"Things could pick up."

"Maybe."

"Brought you chicken soup. Heard you weren't feeling well," Matty said. "Must have had four calls saying Doc Z wasn't herself today."

Zoe didn't meet her eyes. "That's nice of you, but I'm fine." She opened the door and held it for Matty who carried an oversized Thermos. "You want me to bring in your package?"

"It's not my package," Matty said. "Must be for you. Gee, I wonder what it is."

That was sarcasm, since a frame was apparent under the paper of the rectangular package Zoe brought in. She leaned it against the desk chair.

"Funny thing," Matty said, pouring out chicken soup, "Matt called and asked Val to take some pictures at Pegasus Ranch. Real rush job. Something really important."

Zoe made a noncommittal sound.

"If it's any consolation, he doesn't look any better than you do." Matty put a mug in her hands. "Drink your soup and try to get some sleep."

Matty left, but her words by the library back on Beautify Knighton Day remained in Zoe's head as she stared at the wrapped package.

Eventually you realize it's the same person, but it's not the same lesson. You have moved on, you have gotten over that first lesson. But they're here to teach you another one this time.

Zoe emptied the mug and got ready for bed.

She brought the package with her and, sitting up in bed, she tore off the paper and let it drift to the floor.

A close-up of threadleaf phacelia.

She stared at it. Remembering how she'd once stared at that four-word note he'd left.

Blue and white, so bright and crisp it brought tears to her eyes. A flower that bloomed in rugged environs, that conserved water rather than trusting that rain would be plentiful.

She'd never forget the name of this wildflower again. She'd never miss it blooming in the rough country where it thrived.

It's beautiful. Promise you won't just yank it out or poison it because you think it might be bad.

It's just a weed.

It's a wildflower. Every place should have flowers. Especially wildflowers.

He hadn't yanked it out. He hadn't poisoned it. He'd planted one by his door. He'd brought this to her door.

She sat, staring at the colors and lines of the flower. Hearing Kalli's and Val's voices in her head. Thinking of trust and lessons and Matty's switcheroo.

And of Matt.

But not of that night. That one night. Because that was the past. A lesson already learned.

Matt straightened from hooking Thunder to the long leash as Zoe got out of her vehicle. He was on the phone.

His eyes never left her as she slowly approached.

His expression was an odd mix of satisfaction and wariness, but which was for her and which for the phone call he completed as she advanced to the bottom step, she couldn't tell.

"I came for my plate."

"Your plate?"

"You were going to give it to me before, only Thunder had licked it."

"Oh. Right."

"Is this a bad time?" she asked.

"No. Just setting up some business in Cody."

She eyed him. "Now?"

"Not right this minute, no. I'll leave Thunder with Jarrod Malloy tomorrow—no sense taking her to Cody when I'll be in meetings most of the time. I'll leave late afternoon. Stay overnight, do my business in the morning day after tomorrow, then head back as soon as it's wrapped up. Should be back by dinner. If it turns out the way I hope…"

"Bad weather's coming in tomorrow night. Lots of rain. Lots of snowmelt from warmer temperatures. There could be flooding."

"I heard. I'll be across the mountains before it hits and it should be done before I come back." He tipped his head. "Are we gonna talk about the weather?"

CHAPTER TWENTY-EIGHT

He hoped to God her answer wasn't yes, because he thought the weather just might kill him.

Her chin went up and she said, "No. We're going to talk about the photo of the wildflower you left at my door. The scorpion weed."

"Threadleaf phacelia. I asked Val to take the photo."

"Why?"

"Considering how I did with a note, I thought a picture would be better."

"Try talking." She looked up at him, waiting.

"Because it's you," he said.

She blinked. "A scorpion? A venomous creature with claws, which immobilizes its prey in order to eat it."

"No, no, a scorpion *weed.*"

"Oh. Well. A weed. That's fine. A plant nobody wants that overruns the plants people *do* want. Hard to get rid of and—"

He took off his hat and whapped it against the front of his thigh. "*Dammit, Zoe.*"

Two birds skittered away. But Zoe didn't.

"I'm trying to say something here," he added into the silence.

She looked at him.

"Okay." He cleared his throat. "I've thought about this and I can't say I'm sorry I left that night, because if I hadn't I'd probably still be drifting, aimless. But I'll never stop regretting not going back. I had this idea I needed to finish … to show you I'd done what I set out to do before I found you again."

She came up the steps to the porch.

He dropped his hat and reached for her.

She retreated a step.

"No. You are not seducing me and I'm not seducing you, Matt Halderman. Not until we know where we stand."

"Not until?" That sounded like good news, but he wasn't a hundred percent sure. "Does that mean you want to know my intentions? Because that's easy. I intend to marry you."

"You don't have to—"

"The hell I don't. That's what I intend. I'm not saying you have to say yes right this minute, but since not telling you what I was going after screwed things up before, I'm telling you."

Her eyes got misty. "I think you're getting the hang of this talking stuff, cowboy. But now it's my turn." She wrapped her arms around her waist as if to keep them from doing something else. "I had it wrong, Matt. That night in Cody, I put it all on you, thinking it was about trusting you. I practically crammed my trust down your throat."

"I wasn't complaining."

"You should have been. You were short-changed. Because it's about trusting *me*. *My* judgment. Not going on a hope and a prayer that you are who you say you are, but seeing who you are through clear eyes, built up layer by layer from what you do. So you don't just get a shallow 'I trust him because I love him.' You get the full course 'I want him because I can trust him and because he's building a horse hospice and because he's afraid of my grandmother and because he's a sucker for a puppy and because he planted a wildflower and because he was good to a kid having an asthma attack and a hundred other reasons.' "

"Can we go back some? To where you've applied your good judgment and clear eyes and all and you—"

She stepped into him. "Want you. If you want me."

He wanted her.

The first touch nearly did it.

He got her inside, but no farther, backing her against the door, unbuttoning with one hand, sliding her shirt down with the other, so he could kiss, and taste. Drawing down her straps to expose that sweet, silky curve.

She made that hum. And he tried to capture it with his open mouth.

It deepened. He liked that even better.

She had her hands on his belt, the zipper, him.

They both groaned.

"The bedroom…" she said.

"Here." He opened her jeans and pushed them down.

"Here? Can you hold me?"

"Oh, yeah."

If she had doubts, she had a strange way of showing them, because she'd toed off her shoes and was wiggling out of her jeans and all, with an urgency that nearly undid him.

He kissed and sucked wherever he could find her, while he pulled on protection with hands that seemed to have forgotten the first thing about the procedure.

"Are you…?" He slid a finger gently along her, into her.

She moaned. "Yes. Yes."

He hooked her one knee in the crook of his elbow, she wrapped the other leg around his waist. He dipped his knees and came into her.

They stilled.

The rhythm of their breathing, the flutter of their muscles became the lightest of thrusts. Building from where they joined.

Spreading. Deepening.

He heard her cry, felt the first waves of release taking her, pulling him.

It came fast then. Fast and complete.

"Bedroom" was the first word he managed.

"Put me down and—"

"I'm not putting you down. I'm not letting you go."

"Um. I think Thunder's still outside."

That's what that noise was.

He swore and let her down gently. "Don't go anywhere."

He closed his jeans, slid out the door to unhook Thunder and bring her in.

Zoe had picked up her discarded clothes. Something about the way she stood there with them bundled against her…

"Around my waist," was all he said before he picked her up fast.

She had her arms around his neck, her legs around his waist immediately.

Matt started for the bedroom.

Thunder danced around excitedly.

The short distance across the open space wasn't too bad, but as he started down the hallway, Thunder began to bark and make darting raids for the hem of his jeans.

"She thinks it's a game," Zoe said, laughing.

"Quit encouraging her," he grumbled. "Thunder. Stop."

His shoulder hit the wall on one side, he stepped, thought he felt the dog under foot and stumbled into the other wall.

They finally reached the bedroom doorway.

"Thunder. Sit. Stay," he ordered.

The puppy sat, looking at him expectantly.

"No way are we making this a three-way," he muttered.

Zoe chuckled into the side of his throat.

He kicked at the door with one foot, didn't get it all the way closed. Zoe loosed one arm just long enough to push until it clicked. Thunder yipped her displeasure.

He carried Zoe to the side of the bed.

"That didn't turn out to be the romantic gesture I'd hoped for."

Zoe kissed his throat, then slid down his body, dropping her clothes and opening his jeans. "It's plenty romantic."

In the bed, their clothes gone, he paused and looked down at her.

"I'm not going anywhere, Zoe. Not this time. I'll be here when you wake."

She caught her breath. Then she blinked. "It's your house. Of course you won't go anywhere."

Everything suspended for an instant. Then he laughed. Or they both laughed together.

Because they were certainly both laughing when their mouths came together. Laughing and panting and murmuring.

CHAPTER TWENTY-NINE

Matt came back to the bed and scooped her to him.

Thunder whined outside the once-again-closed door.

"Poor little thing. Is she hungry?"

"She's eaten. And been out. Twice," Matt said into her throat, wondering if he could capture that humming sound again. And again. "She wants in here."

"You don't want to let her in?"

"I've been letting her sleep in bed with me. She'd want to join us."

Zoe craned her neck to stare at him a moment. "Okay. I can live with the crying for tonight."

"Training starts tomorrow," he promised, pulling her on top of him, finding his place in her as she arched back and sighed his name.

The phone woke her. Hanging partway off the bed, she groped for her bag on the floor.

"It's mine," Matt said, kissing her bare hip. "Go back to sleep."

Hazily, she was aware of him pulling on jeans one-handed as he listened to the phone.

She drifted for a while. But there was something in the tenor of his voice that snagged her attention. It wasn't the words. She couldn't hear them.

Or maybe it was the scent of coffee. If there was food to go with that coffee…

They'd microwaved the last of the stew Matty had brought and Matt had frozen. But that had been hours ago.

Matt's shirt, the blue plaid one he'd worn on Beautify Knighton Day, was on her side of the bed, so she put that on and followed sound and scent to the kitchen.

Thunder pranced over to her with a chew toy. Matt gave her a heated look, then poured out a mug of coffee and handed it to her while he listened to the phone.

"… Yes. I'll be there. See you then."

Matt clicked off, leaned back against the sink and grinned.

She grinned back. She couldn't help it. Not with satisfaction radiating from him. "Good phone call?"

"The best. Finalizing details before I go to Cody to do the paperwork. But it's all agreed to now, so I can tell you. I'm buying back the H Bar H. All of it. Back in Halderman hands."

She stopped with the mug at her lips.

"That's been my goal from the start," he said. "What I've been working for since looking in that bathroom mirror and knowing I'd drifted too damned long. I set aside money to make it happen whenever I had the chance. Never thought it would come this fast but thanks to Harold—"

"But the Malloys. How can—?"

"The wife is leaving him and wants her share out of the ranch. He has to sell to pay her. And I'm buying."

Jarrod's parents splitting up. That's what had been bothering him the other day. He might not have known the details, but he knew some. And now? The ranch he loved…

"Jarrod," she said.

"Sounds like he's staying with his dad."

"Staying with Connor… But where will they go?"

Matt's grin was gone. "The H Bar H is Halderman land. It was in my family for generations."

"It's been Malloy land for all of Jarrod's life."

"Never should have been. Never should have left Halderman hands."

"It's his home. He's a boy … a boy who would be heartbroken to leave it."

"That's his mother's doing, not mine."

"Oh, Matt. Don't you see? You're not punishing your mother. She won't even notice. But you *will* be contributing to making a boy go through just what you went through and for what? It won't bring your father back. It—"

"I'm not crazy. I don't think—"

"—won't change anything that's happened in your life. It's not where love lives."

His hands tightened on the chair back. "How do you know—? Kalli—?"

"Yes. And you. Humming it all the time. But you should have listened to the words, Matt. Because it's not the house where love lives, just like it's not the H Bar H. The *people* are where love lives. The people." She looked up at him. "Me, Matt. *I'm* where love lives."

"I know you are, Zoe. But it'll be even better on the H Bar H. It's what I've been working for since that night with you and meeting Harold. You with your goals that nothing could stop you from achieving. Harold with what he said about loving and life. I knew I needed to get back to the H Bar H. That was the reason for the business. Why I worked so hard. Why Harold left me the money. He said it in a letter. And now it's all coming together. You, me, the H Bar H—"

"Jarrod Malloy."

They looked at each other for a long moment.

She knew this was wrong. Wrong for him. But she couldn't pull the right words together. Couldn't sort through the emotions and tugs of the past twenty-four hours to gather the few perfect words to make him see.

Her phone rang from the bedroom. She reached it just in time. A rancher at the northern tip of Lewis County had cut himself badly.

She pulled on the clothes she could find as she listened. She hung up as she returned to the main area. Her shoes were by the door.

Heat flooded through her at the memory—more than a memory, more like sensations relived—of him holding her, of him inside her.

She pulled the shoes on, making her shaky hands work. Then she went to him, where he leaned back against the sink, his expression so different now.

"I have to go. Matt." She placed her hand on his chest. "Please, don't do anything yet. Can't we talk about this later?"

"I'm going to Cody, Zoe. It's done."

CHAPTER THIRTY

Zoe tugged her hood up, tucked the backpack under the rainproof poncho, and jogged from her vehicle into the clinic.

Still her pants were soaked from her knees to where they tucked into her waterproof boots.

"It's a deluge out there," she told Polly. "They're reporting the storm's not moving any time soon."

At least the weather gave her something to think about other than Matt.

Was he over the mountains by now? Unless he'd decided not to go. If he'd changed his mind—

"Same in here," Polly said. "Deluge downstairs from the rain and upstairs from the phone calls. This is what we get for wanting spring weather."

"Basement's flooding?" She hung her poncho where its dripping would do the least damage.

"Yup. Hugh's down with Doc seeing what needs to come up. Most calls are cancelling and rescheduling." The phone rang. "But this stack's for you."

She handed over messages with one hand and answered the phone with the other.

After nearly two hours, Zoe had worked through the original stack, while Polly added more. It kept her mind occupied. Her heart wasn't as lucky.

"It's going to flood down there for sure," Hugh said, bringing up boxes from the basement.

"Only way it'll get cleared out," Polly called from the front.

Doc Johnson grumbled, but low enough that she wouldn't hear.

They were discussing where to put the boxes when Polly appeared in the doorway. "Earl's on the phone. He thinks he broke his leg and wants somebody to go up there to him."

Matt had crossed the Big Horns before the worst weather hit, as he'd predicted. Though, even on the relatively flat belly of the Big Horn Basin between the mountains and Cody, the worst was plenty bad enough.

Events from this morning replaying in his head didn't help.

It's his home. He's a boy … a boy who would be heartbroken to leave it.

That's his mother's doing, not mine.

Oh, Matt. You're not punishing your mother. She won't even notice. But you will be contributing to making a boy go through just what you went through and for what?

It would put right things that had gone so wrong. The H Bar H was Halderman land. That's what for.

But were new wrongs being done?

Taking Thunder to the home ranch for Jarrod to look after hadn't been easy. The kid had been crying.

Connor Malloy had said he wasn't going to tell his son until everything was done, so the tears must have been about his mother leaving.

That meant Jarrod still greeted Matt as a friend.

He supposed that would change soon.

It's not the H Bar H. The people are where love lives. The people.

By the time he arrived in Cody, Matt was more than ready for dinner, a hot shower, and an early night.

Except his managers put him in the room where he and Zoe had spent that night. Most of that night. Not enough of that night. He'd avoided it since, but the place was otherwise full. So there he was. Back at the beginning.

In the shower he almost thought he could see Zoe coming out of the steam. Reaching for him.

In bed, it was worse. Last night and that first night blended and blurred. Neither allowed him much sleep. When he did sleep he dreamt of a wildflower.

It was still dark when he gave up. Might as well get ready.

Pulling a clean shirt from his bag, the envelope from Harold's lawyer fluttered out.

He drew out the handwritten note.

From the first, I have greatly enjoyed our talks, Matt. I am proud of you for what you have accomplished in such a short amount of time through your hard work. And you should be, too.

What I wish most for you now is that you find what is right for you.

Use this money for what you most want, Matt.

I trust your good judgment to know what that is.

He'd been so sure when he first read it. It had all seemed so obvious. The H Bar H. The horses. Make things right. Simple and clear.

Find what is right for you…

What you most want…

Zoe standing in front of him, wearing only his shirt. Her eyes on him. Those eyes…

Me, Matt. I'm where love lives.

Matt came out of the lawyer's office in Cody, wishing lawyers didn't use twenty words when one would do. Two and a half hours, when all he wanted was to get on the road.

His next stop was the bank. Just under an hour. Still too much. But at least it was done.

He turned his phone on as he ducked into his truck out of the rain. Nothing from Zoe.

Maybe that was too much to hope for, but there was another number from Knighton he'd expected to see. One he'd spent a lot of time on the phone with in the first hours after re-reading Harold's note.

There was, however, a series of calls from Walker. Strange, since they'd said what needed saying before he'd started his business this morning.

He hit Walker's number without listening to the messages.

"You're still in Cody?" was Walker's greeting.

"Yeah. Wrapped things up. About to head back."

"Roads across the Big Horns are closed. You'll have to go around."

"Damn. I'll have to go up to Billings, then swing south." That would add an hour.

"This storm's sitting west of Knighton." West of Knighton was the mountains, where steep slopes, narrow canyons, and rocky ground were an incubator for flooding. Walker didn't have to say that. They both knew it. "It's dropping slushy snow up top, but it's raining high enough up to add to the snowmelt from the warmth."

"What are you? The National Weather Service?" Matt tried to make it light, but he didn't like what he was hearing. Or seeing. No messages or calls from Knighton. "Have you heard if communications are out?"

"No, but it wouldn't surprise me. I'll call if there's news."

As soon as they disconnected, he tried Zoe's number. Unavailable.

He tried another number, got the same message. Also for the clinic. Taylor and Cal. Dave and Matty. Jack Ralston. The diner. He even tried Ruth and Hugh Moski. If they answered, he'd gladly give up the piece of his hide they'd likely take.

They didn't. Nobody answered.

Matt's detour soured fast.

There was an accident. No serious injuries to people. Vehicles were another matter. It was an hour before traffic could get past. The rain never quit, but daylight did.

All attempts to call to Knighton got the same "unavailable" message.

Just past Billings, Walker called again. "They've closed I-90 south of Sheridan."

"Other roads—"

"Closed. They're reporting Knighton's cut off."

"There's got to be a way—"

"This storm's holding in place. The weather people say it's real unusual. It's bringing the snowmelt down like a tidal wave. There's a lot of flooding."

"I've got to—"

"No, you don't. Sometimes you got to sit back and wait. That horse laugh you hear in the background is my wife saying things about pots and kettles." Despite himself Matt felt his mouth ease. Not a grin, but less of a grimace. "Stop in Sheridan. Get a room, some sleep. Be fresh to help when you can get in."

The Road Closed sign was enforced by portable metal gates, construction barrels, and a state trooper.

Matt swore as he exited. He swore more when he found the closest motel full. At the next one, the desk clerk was telling him they were sold out when a familiar voice said from behind him, "My room's got two beds, Matt."

Dave Currick.

He'd flown in to Billings earlier and encountered the same road-blocks—on the highway and with communication—as Matt had.

"They'll be okay," Dave said during their late dinner in the jammed hotel restaurant. "They've got good heads on their shoulders, they won't take risks, and they'll help each other out."

Matt agreed with the good heads and helping each other out, but would Zoe put herself at risk to help a patient? To help anybody? Hell, yes.

"Besides, you're better off than I am," Dave said. "I took a car to the airport. Even after they open the interstate, I'll have issues."

"You can ride with me."

"Done."

Zoe parked behind the clinic in barely-there dawn and expelled a long-held breath.

There'd been times… But she had made it. Up to Earl Krenetz's mountain cabin and down, with preliminary treatment for his leg in between. Slipping, sliding, and detours, but made it. He was now in the hospital at Jefferson, which was running on a generator.

She got out and stretched, disregarding the steady rain. It would feel good to sleep. And to be dry.

Polly was asleep in her chair behind the reception desk with another chair pulled up as an ottoman. She sat up and turned a flashlight on Zoe.

"About time you got back." Polly said it with enough tartness to know she'd been worried. "Thought your grandparents were going to drive me crazy."

"My grandparents? Have they been calling?"

Polly snorted. "We haven't had phones since right after you left. A few folks wandered in for Doc to patch up, but—"

"Zoe?" Ruth came out of Exam Room 1 looking rumpled and tired.

"Grandma? What are you doing here?"

"Waiting to see that you're okay, of course."

"Oh, Grandma." She hugged her. Then hugged Polly, too.

"Well, don't quit, now that you're started." Her grandfather came out of Exam Room 2 looking very much as his wife did. They must have been sleeping—or trying to sleep on the exam tables.

Doc Johnson came out of the office, sleep wrinkles added on one side of his face to his usual assortment. "Told you she'd be fine."

"What's been happening? Town doesn't look too bad."

"Basements all have water," Ruth reported. "The diner was threatening to flood bad, but folks pitched in and improvised sand bags. Started to recede about four. That garage of Ervin Foley's finally fell down. Roads are out, especially north. At least three dams have failed."

"How do you know all this if communications are still out?"

"A few texts came in," Polly said.

"Texts," Ruth snorted. "Old-fashioned word of mouth. Passed from neighbor to neighbor as they checked on each other. Share the news and pass it on."

A phone rang. Sharp and unexpected.

"Worst dam breach sounds like one up in Lewis County," Hugh said. "Took out a chunk of the highway this side of Taylor and Cal's place."

"Near the H Bar H?" she asked quickly. Matt's place sat lower than much of the surrounding land.

"Jarrod Malloy for you." Polly handed Zoe the phone.

CHAPTER THIRTY-ONE

"Hey, Jarrod, are you okay?" Zoe left gaps between her words, listening to his breathing. "Did you make it through the storm okay?"

"Dad and I are okay. It's Matt's horses."

He sounded good. She started to relax, then his final words sank in. "Matt's horses?"

"That dry creek bed? It's all flooded. The main pasture's a lake. The horses are all up on that knoll. There's hardly room for them, but it's the only dry spot. They're stranded. Dad and I were out in the pickup, checking our place and saw them. But we can't get to them in the truck."

She heard Connor Malloy's voice in the background, but not his words.

"Dad's getting stuff together. Says we'll have to go on horseback. It's bad, Doc Z. Water's rising and they're not moving. Scared of all the stuff in the water."

"It'll be okay. We'll bring help. Just—Jarrod? Jarrod? Are you there?"

The line had gone dead.

Zoe quickly relayed Jarrod's information. She looked at her grandparents and Doc Johnson, knowing how tired they were. "You all stay here and I'll—"

"No," her grandmother interrupted. "Doc stays here in case anyone comes who needs medical attention. Polly, you find Deputy Jessup to get him to use emergency communication to put out a call, then come back here and see if the phones—"

"I'll text everybody, too. Texting might come back first."

"—are working. Meantime, Hugh and I will split up and play Paul

Revere. I'll start with the Curricks at the Slash-C, then work south. Hugh, you get Cal first, then on from there."

"Yup," he said. "If we get those folks, don't hardly need anybody else."

"Get everybody you can," Zoe said. "I'll go straight there and connect with the Malloys. Be careful driving. It's muddy and—"

"Us? You be careful, girl. We've been driving these roads in all kinds of conditions before they were even roads."

They finally opened the damned road. But not until mid-morning.

The rain had let up, but there were reports of flooding. A lot of flooding.

Getting off the interstate meant slow going, with unexpected patches of mud, trees and brush occasionally intruding, and two areas where sludge seeped across. Matt took those slow, since they might hide broken pavement.

He was easing the truck through the second when Dave's phone rang.

"Matty. Everybody okay? … Good, good. … Yeah, fine. I'm with Matt Halderman, in his truck. We put up at the same motel last night when they closed I-90. We'll have to go back and get—…"

Dave glanced toward him. Matt felt that look but kept his eyes on the road.

"Yeah… Yeah, okay. I will. But you be careful and—Matty? Matty?" Dave swore. "It's died again."

"Everybody's okay, so what was Matty's bad news?" He'd reached the far side of the washover and spared a glance at Dave.

"Zoe?"

"Yeah. She got everybody to your place. A dam broke. That dry creek bed's flooded and your horses are cut off. They're on high ground now, but they're spooked. Water's still rising and it's carrying a lot of debris. They're going to try again. Thing is, they've heard another dam might go."

Matt pressed his foot down on the accelerator.

"Can't get in by the ranch road anymore, Matt. We'll have to go in from the north, so we'll have to—

"Too long."

"Matty said the ranch road isn't passable and—*Tree*," Dave called out.

A fallen tree blocked the road ahead. Matt slowed some.

Dave said, "The two of us might be able to move it. Or get ropes around it and use the truck—"

"Forget that. Going around."

Matt swung left past outstretched branches, felt the shoulder give slightly under the truck's left wheels. He guided the nose of the truck back toward the center of the road. Branches screeched along the truck's flank.

The shoulder was going. He could feel the back left tire start to slide toward the muddy ditch.

He accelerated, steady but hard. The truck lurched, as if trying to hold on. And then that left rear tire found purchase from somewhere and the truck leapt forward.

He fought the wheel to keep from shooting across the road into the opposite ditch. Still, the truck was fishtailing, before he had all the motion going the direction he wanted to go—had to go. The accelerator down again.

"You do know you won't do any good if you kill yourself, don't you?" Dave asked mildly. "Not Zoe, not anybody."

He said nothing.

They were close. Nearly to the H Bar H Ranch road.

In sight now.

Damn.

The ranch road was a rushing stream. The only good news was that the highway past where the ranch road came in was downhill, so the water was going that way, not into this stretch of highway. It wasn't just water, though. Mud, branches, a fence post, what appeared to be barbed wire, and more.

A sheriff's department car sat sideways across the road. The figure in the slicker waving at them to turn around was Duane Jessup.

"Deputy Jessup is ordering you to stop," Dave pointed out.

Matt muttered a curse.

They still had a few hundred yards of pavement before they reached the improvised river. Matt studied the ditch and bank beside the road.

"I'll also say I won't be too pleased if you kill me," Dave said mildly. "Not to mention what Matty would do to you if you survive."

There was silence for a second, then Dave added, "Possibly even if you don't survive."

"Then hang on. Because here we go."

Matt took the ditch at an angle, churning along its muddy side for a moment, then turned the nose uphill. The tires spun, spraying mud, digging for purchase. But if they dug too deep…

A tire grabbed, swinging the nose back toward the bottom of the ditch. He fought back, holding on, trying to get that purchase to work for him, balancing, calculating.

Just like on a bronc or bull.

Only this was the roughest ride of his life. This was the one that counted.

Another wheel caught, they were climbing, sliding sideways, then climbing again.

Dave muttered something, possibly a prayer, possibly a curse. Then asked, "How're you going to get through the fence?"

Fence stretched parallel to the road, leaving just enough room for the pickup to stay out of the ditch. But that room would run out, because the fence didn't quit until it reached the torrent of muck and debris coming toward them down the ranch road.

Matt aimed for the section that connected the fence to the high post that held the H Bar H name in an entry arch.

He ignored Jessup yelling, from behind them now. He brought his foot down hard on the accelerator and punched through the fence, then yanked the wheel to the right to keep from going into the flooded ranch road.

He angled the truck across pasture toward Pegasus Ranch.

"How'd you know you could get through there?" Dave kept a good grip on the bar beside his head, though this was easier driving. Not smooth, but easier.

"I strung that fence as a kid. Last summer before Dad died. Never was much good at fencing. Surprised it's still standing."

Dave gave a short laugh. Then he said, "They've got trailers and trucks and equipment up on that high ground behind the house. And it looks like most of the horses are in a rope corral there, but… Two riders are going back into the water toward the knoll. Jack and Zoe."

CHAPTER THIRTY-TWO

Matt drove past the house, nearly to a knot of people holding the reins of their saddled horses.

He brushed past questions from all around to reach the spot where the water edged ever higher. It was as close as he could get to the knoll.

"Took two tries, but we got most of them," Matty told them as she hugged Dave. "The second time, they followed our horses once we got them started, and brought them out. The news might not be as good about the barn and house, Matt, because that's the way the water's rising. But Jack and Zoe think they can save that last horse…"

He could see two horses with riders in the murky water, approaching the knoll. A single horse remained higher up the slope.

"She came back to get Thunder," Taylor said from his other side. "See her? Crossways, in front of Zoe."

Zoe was riding with the puppy across her lap. A squirmy, yipping, distraction in a situation that required concentration and—

"We rigged Thunder in a life jacket and hooked her so she can't wiggle much."

"Why the hell did she take the dog—?"

Then he knew.

The single horse was a sorrel.

Python.

A horse as mean as a snake.

He'd lash out, bite Roo, who'd jump just like his name, unseat her. She'd be in that treacherous, tainted…

"Give me a horse." He looked around for a mount.

Cal Ruskoff held his arm. He tried to shake him off. "She's got this,

Matt. She's got it. Watch."

He turned back to the scene.

Zoe was so still, as if she didn't even exist. Just the horses and the dog. Smart.

Jack had circled wide, coming in well behind Python. Close enough for the horse to feel the pressure, far enough back not to panic him.

Matt could almost imagine he heard Thunder yipping, though the noise of the rushing flood had to be masking it.

Roo slowly turned, easy and relaxed. Zoe had to look ahead for hazards from branches and bushes and other detritus carried by the water. That put her back to Python.

Python tossed his head. For an instant … but, no, he was moving. No longer frozen. But if something happened, Zoe would have no warning—

"They've got it," Cal murmured. "He's following her."

Matt didn't take his eyes off Zoe, Thunder, and Roo for each step of their journey, but he heard the comments of the others around him.

About Zoe going into the mountains in the worst of the storm for a man with a broken leg.

About her gathering all these people to rescue the horses.

About her leadership in escorting the main herd to safety.

And then he could breathe again. Because farther upstream, Roo stepped out of the water, heading toward the rope corral. Still steady, unhurried, calm. Python followed, with Jack still behind.

Several of the volunteers escorted Python inside the corral with great caution.

Matt had covered half the distance between them when Zoe turned Roo and saw him. She smiled.

She was still smiling when she came up beside him.

He reached up and took her by the waist, drawing her off Roo.

"Hey. What—?"

Hands took Roo's reins, more unhooked Thunder, and several pairs seemed to be pushing him and Zoe to the side, out of the way. That was fine with him.

"You were crazy going out there for—"

"Python wouldn't come for me." She looked exhausted, yet her eyes were bright. "But he came for Thunder. I wasn't sure it would work, but it did. We did it, Matt. We got them all to safety."

"—a mean-as-a-snake horse."

"I handled it. You think you could have done better?"

"Hell, no." That made her blink. "I'll tell you this, Dr. Zoe Parisi, if I see you do a fool thing like that again I'll have a lot more to say. And from what I hear that's not even the worst you did during this storm. Going up that goat track Earl calls a road. When the telemedicine program starts, you're not going up there ever again. If Earl Krenetz breaks a leg, he can just fix it himse—"

"That's ridiculous and you know—What? What do you mean when the telemedicine program starts?"

"July. Since it's paid for now."

"Paid? But, how—? You? *You*…? But—"

"Harold's note said to use the money for what I most want. I kept thinking that was getting the H Bar H back. I'd told Harold in the diner—about my dad, the ranch, and his dream of taking in old horses. But I also talked about you. And Harold told me about his wife and how wonderful that kind of love was. He told me to go back to you that night to see if we had a chance. I told him I couldn't. Not as long as I was only moving away from things.

"But when I read his note again yesterday morning, there was this one line: 'What I wish most for you now is that you find what is right for you.' And I knew—I *knew*—he wasn't talking about the ranch or the horses. He was talking about you. You're what's right for me, Zoe. And I'll do my damnedest to be what's right for you."

"But the ranch. *Your* ranch."

"Yeah. About that, I should find Connor Malloy." Later. For the foreseeable future, he had no inclination to look anywhere but at her. "Have some details still to work out, since we were winging it this morning, but the bottom line is I bought out his wife's share, so he and Jarrod will stay where they are. That left enough for the telemedicine program, combined with Cal's foundation match."

"Oh, Matt." She took a step toward him, then stopped. "But the horses. All the work you've done."

"I'll still do the hospice here on Pegasus. I just won't own all of the H Bar H."

A rumbling, cracking, clattering sound reached them.

"Everybody back! Everybody back!"

"The barn's going."

"Stand clear!"

They turned to see the old wooden structure half slide, half crash into the flood.

Dust and water spray obscured the view, taking long moments to subside enough to see.

"Hey, it's routing the water away from the house." That sounded like Taylor's voice.

"Most good that thing has done in decades," Cal said.

"Gulch was right about it not lasting till fall. Looks like we'll be doing a barn-raising instead of barn-repairing," Dave said from the other side of Zoe. He slung an arm around her shoulders. "Zoe, a little later, I'll tell you about the drive I just took with this guy and you'll have all the ammunition you'll ever need if he brings up you taking risks."

"Oh?" Zoe slanted a look up at Matt. "Is that so?"

"Hey," he protested. "What happened to the solidarity of men?"

"Went out the window when you took me on the ride of my life— and nearly my death."

"What's this?" Matty asked, joining them.

"Not a thing, dear." Dave transferred his arm to his wife, kissing the top of her head.

They walked off together.

"What was that about?" Zoe asked.

"I think that was Dave saving me from certain death at the hands of Matty at the same time he put my life into your hands. If you'll have it."

She looked up at him, eyes wide, but said nothing.

"I won't rush you, Zoe. But when a man finally figures out where love lives, he—"

"Shut up and kiss me, Halderman."

"I can do that."

He kissed her.

He kissed her long and deep.

Not as long or as deep as he'd like. But it would hold him for a while. At least until he could get her alone and take turns doing the seducing.

He wrapped his arms around her and squeezed.

"Hey, I can't breathe," she protested, then proved herself a liar with a laugh that tickled his ear.

He spun her around, lifting her feet off the ground. Two, three times. Possibly four. When he stopped he was looking at the horizon. Those pieces of rock meeting sky in the particular way that would always mean home to him.

We did it, Dad. We really did it.

He thought of two more good men who'd taught him lessons of love. Walker Riley and Harold Hopewell.

And then he laughed at the thought of a few more men, the ones who'd dragged him into a shop named Flower Power.

"We're just starting, Zoe. Just starting. Now that we know where love lives."

If you enjoyed Where Love Lives, I hope you'll consider leaving a review, to let your fellow readers know about your experience.

For news about upcoming books, subscribe to Patricia McLinn's free newsletter.

www.PatriciaMclinn.com/newsletter

The Wyoming Wildflowers series

Donna and Ed's lives are worlds apart.
Can they ever bridge the distance…
Wyoming Wildflowers: The Beginning

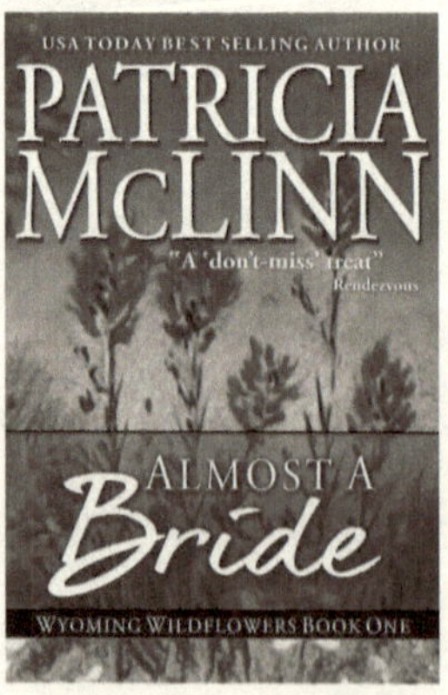

Dave Currick has everything he wants,
except the woman he loves…
Almost a Bride

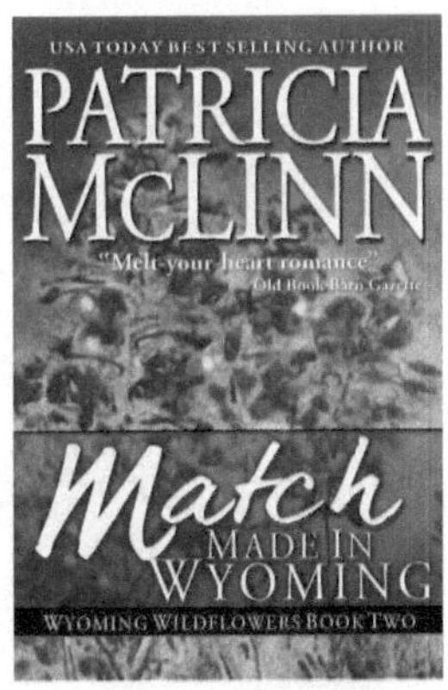

Cal and Taylor can spark a wildfire,
but will they come together in …

Match Made in Wyoming

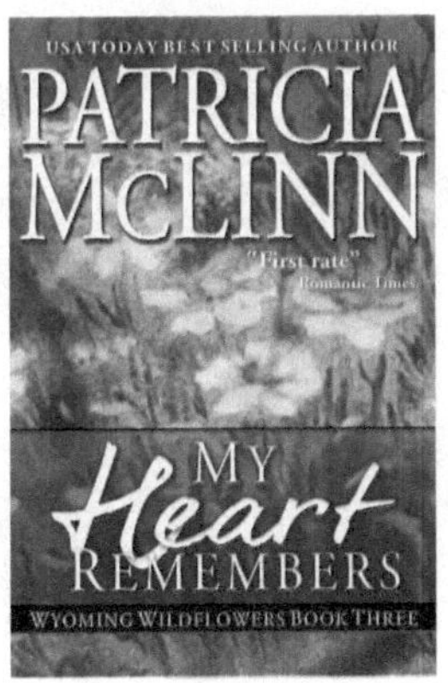

Lisa Currick's carried a secret in her heart for years—
and he just hit town …

My Heart Remembers

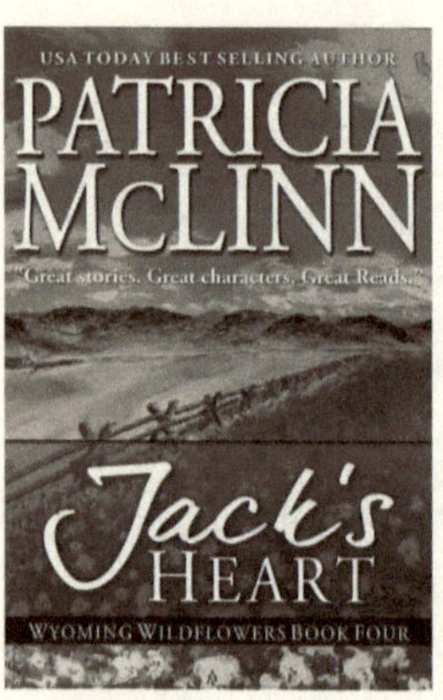

Jack's Heart brings emotional impact
to this romantic comedy.

Jack's Heart

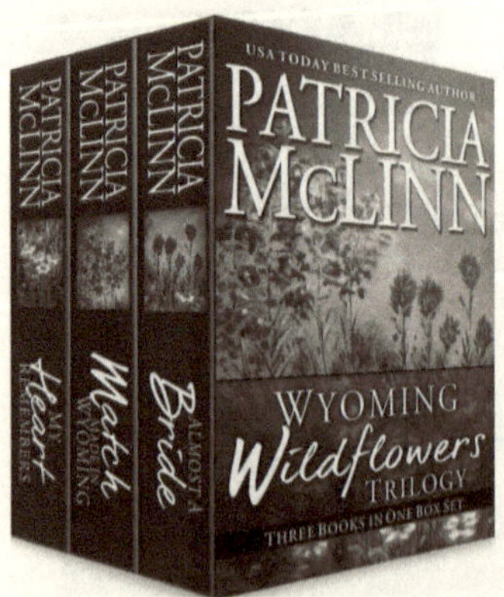

Or read the three books for one great price
in the Wyoming Wildflowers boxed set …

Wyoming Wildflowers Trilogy Boxed Set, 3 Books in 1

What people are saying about the
WYOMING WILDFLOWERS series

"If you've been feeling burned out and let down by category romance, the Wyoming Wildflowers series will remind you how much there is to love in the genre."

—Writers Club Romance Group on AOL

"While the mystery itself is twisty-turny and thoroughly engaging, it's the smart and witty writing that I loved the best."

—Diane Chamberlain, bestselling author

"I was touched by the love described in this series. Ms. McLinn is the real deal writer. So satisfying."

—Amazon 5* review

If you particularly enjoy connected books—as I do!—try these:
A Place Called Home series
The Bardville, Wyoming series
The Wedding Series

Explore a complete list of all Patricia's books
patriciamclinn.com/patricias-books

Who's Who in the
Wyoming Wildflowers series

Contemporary western romance with a touch of humor

The Slash-C Ranch

Ed and Donna (Roberts) Currick

Wyoming Wildflowers, The Beginning, Book 1

Children: Dave, Lisa

Dave and Matty (Brennan) Currick

(Matty's family ranch is the Flying W)

Almost a Bride, Book 2

Chidren: Brennan, Finn

Lisa (Currick) and Shane Garrison

(Live most of the year in New York City)

My Heart Remembers, Book 4

Children: Alexa

Jack Ralston and Valerie Trimarco

Jack's Heart, Book 5

Children: Addison Rose "Addie", Ralston Baby-to-Be

    (Eleanor "El" Thatcher and Cahill McCrae

    Prequel: **A New World**

    Children: Sam)

    Bryan, part-time ranchhand and college student

Ruskoff Ranch

Taylor Anne Larsen and Cal Ruskoff

Match Made in Wyoming, Book 3

Children: Cassie, Rob

Pegasus Ranch

Zoe Parisi and Matt Halderman

Where Love Lives, Book 6

    (Kalli Evans and Walker Riley

    Prequel: **Rodeo Nights**

    Children: Miranda, Jeff, Hayley)

The People of Knighton, Wyoming

Ruth and Hugh Moski

    Grandparents of Zoe Parisi

    Ruth manages Dave Currick's law office on the second floor, above the Van Hopft Pharmacy

    Own apartments, including the second story apartment that has been home to Taylor Larsen, Shane Garrison, and Zoe Parisi.

The clinic

    Doc Johnson

    Dr. Zoe Parisi

    Polly, office manager

    Delva, nurse

Other residents:

    Rainie, Waitress in the Knighton Diner. Married to George, three children

    Reverend Ervin Foley

    Joyce Aberdick, Assistant Manager of the bank

    Deputy Duane Jessup, assigned to the Clark County Sheriff's Department Knighton sub-station

    Mrs. Brontman, "the Widow Brontman"

    Annie Gatchell, works at the library. Married to rancher Terry Gatchell

    Brandy, works at the post office

    Mrs. Van Hopft, former second-grade teacher

    Pamela Dobson, cleans houses in both counties

In Jefferson, county seat of Clark County, biggest town in both counties

    Owner of the Flower Power shop

    Judge Halloran

    Sheriff Kuerten

In Lewis and Clark Counties

    Fred Montress, rancher, briefly separated from wife Betty, now back together

    Terry Gatchell,

    The Pratcher family ranch

    Earl Krenetz, owns small mountain cabin

About the Author

USA Today bestselling author Patricia McLinn's novels—cited by reviewers for warmth, wit and vivid characterization – have won numerous regional and national awards and been on national bestseller lists.

In addition to her romance and women's fiction books, Patricia is the author of the Caught Dead in Wyoming mystery series, which adds a touch of humor and romance to figuring out whodunit.

Patricia received BA and MSJ degrees from Northwestern University. She was a sports writer (Rockford, Ill.), assistant sports editor (Charlotte, N.C.) and—for 20-plus years—an editor at The Washington Post. She has spoken about writing from Melbourne, Australia to Washington, D.C., including being a guest speaker at the Smithsonian Institution.

She is now living in Northern Kentucky, and writing full-time. Patricia loves to hear from readers through her website, Facebook and Twitter.

Visit with Patricia:

Website: patriciamclinn.com

Facebook: facebook.com/PatriciaMcLinn

Twitter: @PatriciaMcLinn

Pinterest: pinterest.com/patriciamclinn

ISBN: 978-1-939215-63-5